Billy reached out and grasped Cody's arm, jerking him to a halt. "Hold on there, mister," he ordered. "We want to palaver with you some more."

Cody cast a glance toward the Gradys, who were still walking. They were cutting through the courtyard in front of the Alamo now. Putting a whining tone in his voice, Cody said, "*Por favor, señores*, I am just a poor old man—"

Fred reached for the brim of the big sombrero. "The hell you are," he muttered. "Let's just have a look at you." He jerked the sombrero off Cody's head and tossed it aside.

Cody was already moving before the hat hit the ground. His left hand grabbed the bottom of the serape and threw it up over his right shoulder, putting the Colt in the clear; his right hand closed around the walnut butt and lifted the gun smoothly from the holster. As Cody cleared leather, Billy yelled, "It's him!" Both of the hard cases reached for their own guns.

They were too slow. Cody squeezed the trigger, then fanned the hammer with his other hand. The Colt boomed twice. . . .

Cody's Law Series
Ask your bookseller for the books you have missed

CODY'S LAW
Volume II

DIE LONESOME

Matthew S. Hart

 Created by the producers of
The Holts: An American Dynasty,
The Badge, and **The White Indian.**

Book Creations Inc., Canaan, NY • *Lyle Kenyon Engel, Founder*

BANTAM BOOKS
NEW YORK • TORONTO • LONDON • SYDNEY • AUCKLAND

CODY'S LAW: DIE LONESOME

*A Bantam Domain Book / published by arrangement with
Book Creations Inc.*

PRINTING HISTORY
Bantam edition / September 1991

*Produced by Book Creations Inc.
Lyle Kenyon Engel, Founder*

*Bantam Books are published by Bantam Books, a division of Bantam
Doubleday Dell Publishing Group, Inc. Its trademark, consisting of
the words "Bantam Books" and the portrayal of a rooster, is Regis-
tered in U.S. Patent and Trademark Office and in other countries.
Marca Registrada. Bantam Books, 666 Fifth Avenue, New York, New
York 10103.*

PRINTED IN THE UNITED STATES OF AMERICA
RAD   0 9 8 7 6 5 4 3 2 1

CHAPTER
1

Cody thought the man was bluffing, but he wasn't sure. He was glad this was just a poker game, not life or death. "I'll call," the tall Texas Ranger said, his dark eyes glinting with anticipation as he tossed a few more chips onto the pile in the center of the baize-covered table. He laid down his hand. Two pair, jacks over treys. Not bad.

Not good enough, he saw a moment later as Axel Farnum, the only other player left in this pot, spread out his cards and revealed three sixes. Farnum grinned and reached out to rake in the chips.

"At least it was somebody else got took this time," muttered one of the other players, a drifting cowhand known only as Pierson.

Cody glanced at him, as did the other men around the table, but nobody said anything. Farnum's eyes narrowed and he let out a grunt. That was his only response, and Cody was glad the rancher decided to let the veiled insult pass. A brawl wouldn't serve any purpose right now.

Cody, Farnum, and Pierson, along with three other men, were sitting around one of the tables in the bar of the Rio Grande Hotel. As Del Rio's leading pleasure palace, not to mention being one of the best-known stops for travelers between Brownsville and El Paso, the Rio Grande always did a brisk business.

At the moment the saloon was so busy that Ernest Palmatier, the proprietor of the place along with his wife, was helping out behind the bar, serving the customers his regular bartenders hadn't gotten to yet. Men stood two deep in places along the long hardwood counter, and all of the tables were full, too. Waitresses in colorful, spangled, low-cut gowns moved among the tables, serving drinks and generally brightening up the room—when they weren't heading upstairs with one of the customers for a few minutes of passion bought with a gold coin. The piano player tried valiantly to provide a counterpoint to the loud talk and laughter that filled the air, but his tinkling melodies were lost for the most part. A blue haze of smoke from dozens of quirlies hung in the air along with the din.

All in all, the Rio Grande was one of Cody's favorite places in the world, and it was as close to home as he had these days. One of the rooms upstairs was always reserved for him, no matter how much his Ranger duties kept him away, and he got to enjoy a friendly game of poker, though he wasn't fanatically devoted to the game the way some men were. An evening spent like this one would normally be relaxing for him.

Tonight was different. Tonight he was working.

Axel Farnum still had the deal, and he was shuffling the cards as Cody, thoughtfully stroking his dark mustache, casually watched him from across the table. The rancher was known to him mostly by reputation. Farnum's Box AF spread to the northeast of Del Rio was a growing, thriving operation, and the man's success showed in his clothing. Rather than the range outfits many cattlemen wore whether they were on their ranches or in town, Farnum sported an expensive gray suit, a starched white shirt, a silk tie, and a cream-colored Stetson now pushed to the back of his head. Cody guessed that Farnum was in his early to mid-forties, ten or twelve years older than himself; his brown hair was showing streaks of gray, and his features were a bit heavy and florid. Not enough work and too many nights in town had softened him somewhat from the rugged stockman who had started the Box

AF several years earlier. But he was still one of the leading citizens of the area.

The man called Pierson was at the other end of the scale—a cowhand who, judging by the looks of him, had never aspired to anything more than forty-a-month-and-found. His clothes were worn and patched, his boots down at the heel, and his hat stained and battered almost shapeless. About the only items he appeared to take good care of were his gun and holster. Appearances could be deceiving, though. Cody had good reason to know that.

"You gonna shuffle them pasteboards all day, or you gonna deal 'em?" Pierson asked, impatience and frustration putting a jagged edge in his voice.

"No need to get in a huff," Farnum said smoothly. He straightened the cards and set them down on the table for the man beside him to cut. Once that was done, Farnum began dealing the next hand.

Cody glanced at his table mates. One of the other men was also a rancher, not as successful as Farnum but with a good spread. His name was Bailey, and Cody knew him slightly. The remaining pair of players were both townsmen, a storekeeper called Clements and a livery stable owner known as Moe. Cody wasn't sure of his last name. None of them were all that important at the moment. Pierson was the only reason Cody was at this table.

The Ranger had been keeping an eye on the drifter for the past few days, trading off with some of the other members of Ranger Company C, which was headquartered here in Del Rio. Captain Vickery, the company commander, had been tipped off that Pierson was tied in somehow with a bunch of wide loopers who had been hitting the local ranchers and then running the stolen stock across the border into Mexico. Of course, such things had a tendency of balancing out—gringo rustlers rode across the Rio at night and came back with plenty of cows belonging to the Mexican ranchers—but the Rangers had to at least make an effort to see if they could put a stop to the situation. Cody didn't know if the *rurales* across the border went to that much trouble, but he suspected they didn't bother.

Still, orders were orders, and if a fella had to work, this was about as pleasant a chore as he was likely to find.

Cody glanced lazily at his cards. Shit. Ten high. He'd keep the ten and the eight, he decided, and toss the small fish back when the time came.

A slight stir in the saloon noise made him glance over his shoulder. A tall, beautiful, redheaded woman in a green gown was coming toward him. Her ample breasts threatened to spill out of the daring neckline as she reached Cody and bent over to run her arms around his neck. Her lips nuzzled his ear, and her white teeth nipped playfully but a bit painfully at the lobe.

"Are you coming upstairs anytime soon, *chéri*?" she asked in a throaty whisper.

Cody grinned, knowing that probably every man in the room was directing an envious stare at him. Marie Jermaine's beauty was legendary in these parts, and though she was hardly Cody's girl alone—anyone who could pay the high price she commanded could have her, after all—Marie made no secret of the man whose company she preferred . . . with no exchange of money necessary.

"Maybe a little later, darlin'," he said easily. He held up the cards. "I'm a mite occupied at the moment."

She pouted prettily. "With a game? If it is games you want, I can show you much better ones that we can play in private. . . ."

It was a mighty tempting offer, but Cody was supposed to keep an eye on Pierson until he was relieved at midnight. That was still two hours away. He sighed. Marie would just have to wait, and so would he.

She clearly knew from the sound of his sigh what his answer was going to be, for, not waiting to hear it, she stood and started to flounce off angrily. But then she paused and looked back over her shoulder, and Cody saw a hint of a smile on her face that told him it was going to be all right. He and Marie understood each other, and sometimes Cody thought that that was more important than the lovemaking they shared.

Farnum's luck continued. He won most of the hands, though Cody or one of the other men would occasionally take a pot. Except Pierson. He lost consistently, and the pile of chips that had been in front of him when the game had begun shrank steadily. The cowhand glowered across the table at Farnum and muttered something under his breath several times, but the rancher continued to ignore him.

Cody was getting bored. The Rangers had been watching Pierson in hopes that he would say or do something to lead them to the rest of the rustlers, but that wasn't likely to happen as long as the man was just sitting here playing poker. And Marie was still hanging around near the table, sometimes watching the game, sometimes sipping a drink, but refusing all the offers that came her way. Obviously she intended to wait for Cody tonight, no matter how long that took.

As a new hand began, Pierson tossed one of his few remaining chips into the center of the table for his ante, then said, "Don't know why I'm still playin'. I always thought poker was supposed to be a game of chance. Chance ain't got nothin' to do with this game tonight."

"You've been mouthing off a lot lately, friend," said Moe, the small, wiry stable owner. "You might have better luck if you'd just watch your cards."

"Nobody asked you to stick your nose in it," Pierson snapped, not taking his eyes off Farnum. "I'm talkin' to somebody else."

A muscle twitched in Farnum's cheek. Pierson's complaints were finally getting to him, Cody decided as he watched with narrowed eyes. Farnum had the deal, as usual. For a second the rancher looked as if he was going to respond to Pierson's taunt, but then he went on with his shuffling.

Just for the hell of it, Cody watched Farnum's hands as he passed out the cards.

A few moments later, as the Ranger riffled out the cards Farnum had dealt him, he saw that he had drawn one of his best hands of the night. He had two pair to start with, sevens and deuces, so even if he didn't get the card he needed for a full house, he would be in good shape.

He was sitting to Pierson's left, and by the time the betting got to him, the stakes had grown considerably, bumped up by the cowhand's raise. Cody stayed, wondering what kind of hand Pierson had drawn.

When Farnum said, "Cards, gentlemen?" Cody threw in the odd jack on his turn and got an eight in its place. He didn't let his disappointment show on his rugged, tanned face. He still had the two pair, after all. Pierson, too, had only taken one card, and the cowboy looked happy for a change. Must've got what he wanted, Cody thought.

Pierson certainly bet as though he was satisfied. By the time play had gone around the table twice more, the pot was one of the biggest of the night, fueled by Pierson's plunging. Cody and Farnum stayed with him, but the other three men gradually dropped out.

The bet was back to Farnum. With a smile, he said, "It had to come down to this sooner or later, I suppose." Carefully, he pushed out exactly the same number of chips as Pierson had left.

Pierson's face flushed. All he could do was call, but if he won, he would more than recoup the money he had lost in the course of the evening. He matched the rancher's bet, saying, "That cleans me out. But you know that, don't you, mister?" He then looked over at Cody.

Cody grimaced. This had gotten out of hand in a hurry. If he raised, he was sure Farnum would match it, and then Pierson would be forced to drop out. He didn't really care if he won or not, but he didn't want Pierson to lose. The cowhand was drawn as taut as a bowstring, and his eyes were hot and shining with anger.

"I call, too," Cody said, throwing in his chips.

Without waiting for Farnum to lay down his hand, Pierson slapped his cards faceup on the table. "Full house," he snarled, "queens over jacks. Beat that if you can!"

Cody shook his head and threw in his two pair. "I can't."

"What about you, Mr. Rancher?" Pierson asked, his voice quivering with hate.

A grin slowly spread across Farnum's face. "There's a lot of royalty staring up from the table, my friend," he said, gesturing toward Pierson's cards. He put his own cards down, one at a time. "All I have are these lowly little hearts. Five of them, to be exact."

Pierson's mouth tightened into a grim line as he stared at the flush. With a laugh, Farnum started to reach for his winnings.

"No!" Pierson cried. Silence fell over the barroom as the patrons turned to look at the commotion.

Cody sat forward slowly, his muscles tense. The other rancher, Bailey, ventured to say, "No need to get upset, Pierson. Axel beat you fair and square."

That was the worst thing he could have said. Pierson countered, "No, he didn't. The bastard cheated me! He's been cheatin' all night!"

The other three men at the table pushed their chairs back and got up in a hurry. Farnum's face reddened as he leaned forward and said quietly, "I'll give you a chance to take back that rash statement, boy."

"I ain't takin' nothin' back!" Pierson shouted. "You're a low-down card cheat, Farnum!"

The rancher's lip curled in contempt, and his right hand darted across his body toward the Colt Cloverleaf he carried butt forward in a belt holster on his left hip. Even as his fingers closed around the grips of the little .41-caliber pistol, Pierson was coming up out of his chair and grabbing for his own gun.

Cody exploded upward, his hands closing on the edge of the table and heaving. It tipped over, chips, coins, and paper money scattering. The Ranger wanted to separate Farnum and Pierson before they could start shooting, and this was the quickest way.

He was a second too late. Pierson cleared leather and fired from the hip, the detonation of the shot deafening even in the big room. Farnum cried out and was thrown backward by the impact of the slug. Out of the corner of his eye Cody saw the rancher falling from his chair, but there wasn't time to see how badly Farnum was wounded. Cody had to stop Pierson before anybody else got hurt.

The drifter was backing up in a hurry, his eyes darting frantically around the room. He turned and took a step toward the door of the saloon, but one of Farnum's ranch hands who had been drinking at the bar yelled, "He shot the boss! Stop the son of a bitch!"

Several more men moved to block Pierson's path. He jerked around, his features contorted in panic, and it was obvious that he had never intended for anything like this to happen. His temper had run away with him, and now an important man lay bleeding on the floor. Escape was clearly the only thing on Pierson's mind.

He lunged to one side, reaching out with his free hand and grabbing the upper part of Marie Jermaine's left arm. His fingers dug cruelly into the soft flesh as he yanked the redhead in front of him.

"No!" Cody shouted. "Let her go!"

"Ever'body just stay still!" Pierson ordered in a loud, hoarse voice. "Me and this gal are walkin' out of here, and nobody better try to stop us!"

Cody's Frontier Colt was in his hand, his fingers tight on the walnut grips. He didn't even remember drawing it. Studying Pierson, he saw the desperation on the cowboy's face. Marie appeared fairly calm, considering the circumstances, but Cody could see the fear in her eyes. *Dammit, Marie,* he said to himself, *why didn't you get out of the way a little quicker?*

No point in thinking about that now. Keeping his voice cool, Cody said, "Just put the gun down, Pierson. Nobody wants this to get any worse than it already is."

Farnum let out a groan from the floor.

"Just stay out of my way, Ranger," Pierson warned. "You think I trust you? Hell, no! I give up, you'll turn me over to Farnum's men for a lynchin' party! The hell with that! I'd rather shoot my way out and die that way!"

That's what it was going to come down to, Cody thought bleakly as he glanced at the Box AF riders. There were a good half dozen of them in the room, and they didn't look as though they were in any mood to make a deal with Pierson, hostage or no hostage.

Cody fastened his gaze on them. "You men clear out," he instructed.

They shook their heads stubbornly. One of them said, "That bastard shot the boss. He's got to pay."

"Goddamn it, this is the Texas Rangers talking!" Cody roared. "Now, clear out!"

They hesitated, shuffling around. There wasn't a man among them who didn't respect the authority of the Rangers, but they had been raised to ride for the brand. That meant sticking up for their boss, no matter what.

Marie took the decision out of anyone else's hands. She moaned and lifted a hand toward her face, as if she were on the verge of fainting. Her hand continued up, and from the pile of red curls on top of her head she snatched a long, sharp hairpin, then jabbed it into the back of the hand holding her other arm.

Pierson screeched in pain and automatically let go of her. Marie flung herself to one side, out of the line of fire, and most of the other people in the room hit the floor as Cody shouted, "Drop the gun, Pierson!"

Cursing fervently, Pierson brought up his Colt and triggered it. He fired three times, but the last two shots went into the floor as he staggered backward, his shirt-front turning red where Cody's bullets had hit him. The Ranger extended his arm, the revolver held steady, and squeezed off another shot. Pierson went down, landing with a thud on the sawdust-covered floor.

Cody drew a deep breath and walked over to the

fallen man, keeping the gun trained on Pierson until he
had kicked the gun out of Pierson's hand. The drifter
was dead, not much doubt about that, but a man didn't
take chances.

An eerie silence had settled over the room after the
thunder of gunshots died away. Cody broke it by turning to Marie and asking, "Are you all right?"

She was picking herself up off the floor, not bothering to wait for anyone to help her. As she brushed the
sawdust from her gown, she said, "Of course I am all
right, *chéri*. Why would I not be?"

But despite her casual tone, her eyes were wide, and
Cody thought she looked like a deer about to bolt. He
knew the feeling. There was nothing good about a gunfight, and he could understand why some of the most
famous shootists in the West had to find a nice dark
alley and puke their guts out after they'd faced down
their latest challenger.

One of these days he'd come up on the short end
himself. Cody knew it, and so did every other man who
lived by the gun. But not tonight. He holstered the revolver, touched Marie lightly on the arm for a second,
then turned to see how seriously Axel Farnum was
hurt.

The rancher had crawled over to the wall next to the
overturned table, where he sat with his back against
the wall. Now that Pierson was dead, some of the other
men in the saloon were getting to their feet, and they
hurried over to cluster around Farnum.

Cody waved them away and said, "Give the man
some room." He knelt in front of Farnum and pulled
the wounded man's coat back. The starched white
shirt had a bright red stain on it high on the right side,
just under the shoulder. Cody studied the location of
the wound for a second, then grunted, "Looks like the
slug might've missed the bone. We can hope so, anyway. Best send for a doctor." He looked up at the faces
crowding in. "Somebody go fetch Doc Johnston. The
rest of you—back off!"

The bystanders muttered among themselves, but

they did as Cody had ordered, going back to the bar and the tables and resuming their drinking and talking. With no one standing close around them now, Farnum looked up at Cody and asked, "How . . . how bad is it, Ranger? You think I'll make it?"

Still kneeling beside the rancher, Cody nodded and said in a low, grim voice that couldn't be heard more than a couple of feet away, "I reckon you will, if that bullet hole doesn't fester. But if you ever try anything like that again while I'm around, I might just kill you myself."

Farnum was already pale from loss of blood, but his taut, sweating features seemed to turn even more ashen. "I . . . I don't know what you're talking about," he protested.

"Sure you do," Cody replied in the same soft voice. "You're nothing but a goddamned cheater, just like Pierson said. You're good at it. Pierson spotted you before I did, and I might not have seen that bottom deal even then if I hadn't been looking for it."

Farnum tried to summon up some wounded dignity to match the wound in his carcass. He said stiffly, "You're insane."

"Nope. Reckon you're the one who's a mite crazy, Farnum. You've got plenty of money, enough to buy and sell a gent like Pierson twenty times over, but still your pride makes you cheat at cards just so you can beat him." The Ranger's eyes narrowed in anger. "You could've got Miss Jermaine killed."

"But I didn't mean—"

"Just shut up," Cody snapped. "Sit there and be quiet until the doctor comes." He straightened, hooking his thumbs in his gun belt and glaring down at Farnum.

He was good and mad, all right, for a couple of reasons. First and most importantly, as he had told Farnum, Marie had been in danger, and the rancher's cheating had been to blame. Cody wasn't going to be quick to forgive that. And secondly, he had been forced to kill Pierson—hadn't been time not to—and the Rangers' possible lead to the gang of rustlers had died along with the drifting cowhand.

On top of that, Pierson had been right, despite the fact that he was a proddy son of a bitch and probably an owlhoot. Tonight Pierson had been the victim, for a change, and it had gotten him killed.

Cody sighed. He wasn't about to waste any tears on Pierson—but he wished things had worked out differently.

Doc Johnston, a tall, gaunt man with graying bushy eyebrows and bristling mustache, came loping into the saloon, looking more like a farmhand than the skilled medico he was. He crossed the room, knelt beside Farnum without asking any questions or sparing more than a glance for the dead man, and began a swift, efficient examination of the rancher's wound. A few moments later Johnston announced, "He'll live."

Sheriff Christian Burke, Del Rio's local lawman, entered the barroom in time to hear that diagnosis. Burke looked mighty relieved to hear the news, Cody thought. The sheriff was five or six years older than Cody, a heavyset, stolid individual with a fondness for good whiskey. Bad whiskey would do in a pinch, too, for that matter. Cody was convinced that the sheriff *wanted* to be a good lawman; he just had absolutely no imagination and very little flair for leadership.

"Heard there was a shootin'," Burke said as he came up to Cody. "Should've figured you'd be mixed up in it. Mr. Farnum get clipped by a stray bullet, did he?"

Cody gave Farnum a cold look. "Something like that." The Ranger nodded toward Pierson's sprawled body. "That gent on the floor took exception to the way the cards were being dealt. The argument might not've amounted to much if he hadn't lost his head. He shot Farnum, then grabbed Miss Jermaine and tried to use her as a shield to get out of here. He didn't make it."

"Can see that," Burke grunted. "Reckon Miss Jermaine and the other folks around here will back up your story, Cody?"

"They saw what happened." Cody looked around when Marie didn't speak up, only to see that she had disappeared. She'd gone on up to her room, he supposed. He couldn't blame her for wanting some privacy after what had almost happened to her.

Marie's testimony wasn't needed, though. At least a dozen men in the room, including Ernest Palmatier, eagerly volunteered to share their versions of the gunfight with the sheriff. Burke listened for several minutes, then nodded his head and waved away the rest of the would-be witnesses. "I don't need to hear the whole thing over again," he said. He raised his voice and asked, "Anybody here want to argue with what's already been said?"

Nobody did, and Burke nodded his head emphatically. "That's that, then. The coroner'll probably want to hold an inquest in the mornin', Cody, but I don't reckon it'll amount to much."

"I'll be there if I can, Sheriff."

From behind them, Doc Johnston asked, "Somebody want to give me a hand here?"

Cody turned to see that the doctor was lifting Farnum to his feet. The rancher's bloodstained shirt had been stripped away, and compresses were tied tightly to his body front and back, where the bullet had come and gone.

"Bleeding's about stopped, but I want to take Mr. Farnum up to my office anyway and do a better job of cleaning those holes," Johnston said. As some of the townsmen gripped Farnum's arms and slid their arms around his waist, the physician warned, "Be careful with him."

Cody stepped over beside Farnum before the men could assist him out of the saloon. "Remember what I told you," Cody said quietly.

The glance Axel Farnum shot at him was full of pure hate. "I'll remember," he promised.

If Doc Johnston or his two helpers noticed the odd-
ness of the exchange, no one said anything. Burke
seemed to miss it entirely. He left the Rio Grande,
along with Farnum, Johnston, and the men half carrying, half dragging the injured rancher.

Some of Ernest Palmatier's employees were setting
the poker table back on its legs, and Palmatier himself
was gathering up the money and chips that had been
spilled on the floor. Miraculously, most of it seemed to
still be there. Very few of the bystanders had taken
advantage of the confusion to grab some coins or
chips, probably because Cody had been standing
nearby with a gun in his hand. Nobody wanted to take
a chance of drawing his wrath.

The thin, gray-haired hotel owner looked up at his
tall friend. "What should I do with all this money,
Cody?" he asked.

"I'll take mine now," Cody said, reaching out to take
approximately the correct amount from Palmatier's
hands, "and divvy up the rest among the other men
who were playing."

"What about Mr. Farnum?"

"I think you'll find when you ask him that he doesn't
want his share. Give it to the others."

Palmatier frowned. "You are sure?"

"I'm sure." Cody's high-crowned hat of soft brown
felt had been sitting on the floor under his chair when
the fracas began. He looked around and spotted the
headgear a few feet away. Luckily, no one had stepped
on it. He picked up the hat, brushing it off, and continued, "If anybody's looking for me, I'll be upstairs.
But it had better be damned important, savvy?"

The hotel proprietor nodded sagely, completely understanding the Ranger's meaning. He bustled off, calling to one of his barmen to go locate the undertaker for
Pierson.

Cody didn't know if Marie would be in her own room
or his. He went into the hotel lobby, gratefully putting
the hubbub of the barroom behind him, then climbed
the stairs and walked along the corridor to his room.

When he tried the knob, it turned easily under his hand. He'd left it locked, but Marie had a key—not that the locks in the hotel would stop *anybody* who really wanted to get in. He had his hand on the butt of his gun as he swung the door open and stepped quickly through the entrance and to one side.

Marie was sitting on the bed. She had taken down her hair, letting the luxurious red curls fall around her shoulders, and taken off the green spangled gown. She still wore her tightly laced corset and silk pantalets. Cody thought she looked beautiful. He kicked the door shut behind him.

"Everything taken care of downstairs?" she asked coolly.

Cody nodded. "Farnum'll be all right." He started to tell Marie about discovering that the rancher had been cheating at cards, but then decided against it. The whys and wherefores didn't matter now. He moved over beside her and put a hand on the soft, warm flesh of her bare shoulder. "That was quick thinking with the hairpin."

She shrugged. "A girl in my line of work learns all sorts of tricks."

Her tone was light and casual, but Cody could tell she was working hard to maintain that pose. She trembled just slightly under his touch, and the smile she gave him as she looked up was just a little too bright and unconcerned.

Cody slid his hand down from her shoulder to her upper arm, took hold of her other arm as well, and pulled her up off the bed. He started to kiss her as he embraced her, but she abruptly buried her face against his broad chest, and her back began to quake as a sob was torn out of her.

For long moments he just held her, his arms tight around her as she cried. Every so often he lifted a hand and stroked her hair. He mouthed meaningless, soothing sounds. As a youngster he'd ridden many a night herd, and sometimes the animals were so spooky, they seemed ready to jump out of their own skins. This was the same thing, in a way. Marie had had ice water in her veins while she was in real danger, but now that it was over and she was safe, she was finally experiencing just how scared, how plain old good and scared, she had been.

Cody knew that feeling, too.

She finally lifted her head and said, "I would not want anyone else to see me this way."

He nodded. "I understand."

"Thank you, Samuel. . . ." Her lips found his.

The kiss started out tender and comforting, or at least that was what Cody had intended. But it got hotter and more demanding in a hurry. Suddenly, neither one of them was interested in anything except getting out of the clothes that were in the way and then falling back onto the bed. The need inside both of them was too great.

The lovemaking didn't last long, but it left them shaken and gasping for breath. And even when it was over, Marie continued to hold Cody as tightly and as close to her as she could. In the small part of Cody's brain that was still capable of coherent thought, he supposed that the danger they had shared tonight was responsible for the undeniable urgency they felt. All the things in life, big and small both, were never sweeter than when they were almost taken away from you, he mused.

And then he buried his face in her sweet-smelling hair and held her even tighter against him and stopped thinking for a while.

CHAPTER

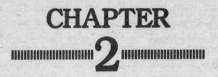

When he was born, his folks had settled the question of what to call him by giving him the names of a couple of favorite uncles and his mother's maiden name. Samuel Clayton Woodbine Cody was a pretty long-winded handle for a little tyke, so he'd become Sam to his parents and his three sisters. He'd signed his Ranger enlistment papers Samuel C. W. Cody. These days, though, Marie was the only one who called him Samuel. With everybody else he answered to Cody.

People watched him when he walked down the street, though he was generally unaware of their interest. He wasn't handsome, but his rugged, tanned features possessed a great deal of strength. His dark brown hair had been lightened somewhat by a life spent in the sun; the full mustache that all but covered his upper lip was a slightly darker shade. Today, like most days, he wore a black leather vest over a blue work shirt, and denim pants tucked into tall black boots. As he sauntered to Company C headquarters, his hat was pushed toward the back of his head, giving him a casual, easygoing appearance. That demeanor changed in a hurry if danger threatened. His brown eyes would narrow and darken, and he would reach for either the Colt on his right hip or the old Bowie on his left that was just as sharp and strong as the day James Black had forged it some fifty years earlier.

The knife was one of several that Black had made for

Rezin and Jim Bowie, and Cody had gotten it from an
old Texan who had sided with Jim in the troubles
around Nacogdoches in '32. Four years later the man
had been part of Houston's army at San Jacinto and
had helped avenge the death of his friend at the Alamo.
After that he had been one of the original Texas
Rangers along with Adam Cody, and eventually he
passed the sturdy, dependable blade down to Adam's
son. Cody knew he was packing history in the leather
sheath on his hip. More importantly, it was a damned
good knife.

Cody nodded to several people as he walked toward
the big adobe-brick building that housed the local
Ranger post. Several of his colleagues were lounging in
front of headquarters, and as Cody came up to them,
one remarked, "Heard tell there was some trouble at
the Rio Grande last night."

"A little," Cody confirmed. "You know how rumors
are, though. Probably made it sound a lot more excit-
ing than it really was."

"Why don't you tell us the straight of it, then?" one
of the others suggested.

"After I've talked to the cap'n. He sent for me."

They weren't going to argue with that. None of them
wanted to get on the wrong side of Captain Wallace
Vickery.

The silver spurs on Cody's boots—part of the legacy
from his father—jingled audibly when Cody strode into
the quiet of the office. Alan Northrup, a stocky Ranger
in his early twenties, was on duty at the desk, a chore
that the younger Rangers drew most of the time. Alan
grinned at Cody and said, "Reckon you've come to see
the captain."

Cody nodded. "That's right."

"He's expecting you. Said to send you right back.
He's all het up about something."

Pausing, Cody frowned slightly. Vickery had a short
fuse to start with. Could be he'd heard about Cody
having to gun down Pierson and was upset about it.

Cody shrugged and went on down the hall. There was nothing he could do to change things now.

"Get on in here!" the captain roared when Cody tapped lightly on his door. Cody walked in, took his hat off, and hung it on one of the nails driven into the wall beside the door. Vickery was at the office window, glowering out at the street.

"Cap'n, if some little old lady walks by, you're liable to scare the sunbonnet right off her, looking like that," Cody said, grinning. "You look like you're fixing to cloud up and rain all over somebody."

Vickery swung away from the window. "I feel like it, too," he growled, walking over behind the scarred desk that had papers scattered across its top. "When the Rangers asked me to come back and be a captain, I never figured they'd try to bury me with all this paperwork!"

Cody's grin widened. Wallace Vickery had never been one for sitting in an office and pushing papers around. In the man's long life, he had fought renegade Indians and Mexican bandits and badmen of every stripe. The only peaceable occupation Vickery had ever had was preaching the gospel, and the way he dished out the hellfire and brimstone made an adventure even out of that. A burly man, Vickery inevitably wore a black broadcloth suit that provided a sharp contrast for his leathery features and snow-white hair and mustache.

"Set yourself down," he grumbled as he began to paw through the welter of documents on his desk. "May take me a minute to find what I'm lookin' for. I swear, Satan must've come up with the idea of fillin' out some damn report for every little thing that comes up. . . ."

Cody settled himself in a ladder-back chair in front of the desk as Vickery kept searching for whatever he was looking for. Breaking into the commandant's mutterings, the younger Ranger said, "I reckon you've heard about what happened at the Rio Grande last

night, Cap'n. I'm sure sorry I had to shoot that fella
Pierson. It just seemed like the thing to do at the
time."

"What?" Vickery's head jerked up. "Pierson? Oh,
yeah, I heard about that." The captain waved a
knobby-knuckled hand. "Hell, don't worry none
about that, son. Praise the Lord nobody else got hurt.
We'll find some other way to dab a loop on them rustlers. I got somethin' more important for you, if I can
just find the dadblasted—" He broke off and tri-
umphantly held up a yellow telegraph flimsy. "Here it
is! Knew I put it here somewhere."

Cody leaned forward expectantly. He hadn't antici-
pated a new assignment this soon, but whatever it was,
he hoped it would get him out of Del Rio for a while.
He had been sitting around town for too long.

"You carry a Winchester '73, don't you?"

The question surprised Cody. Frowning slightly, he
nodded. "Sure. Most of the men do. There's no better
rifle made."

"Somebody sure agrees with you. Couple of weeks
ago, somebody stole over two hundred of 'em from an
army supply depot over there in East Texas."

Cody let out a low whistle. Anyone who got hold of
such a shipment of Winchesters could make a considerable profit on them, especially by selling them to
some of the Indians who were still making life misera-
ble for settlers on the Texas frontier. The thought of
two hundred repeating rifles in the hands of the Comanches made his belly go cold.

"Yep," Vickery agreed, "it's a hellacious situation.
This telegram's from Major Jones over in San Antone.
He's askin' for our help."

That came as a surprise to Cody, too. Major John B.
Jones, head of the Rangers' Frontier Battalion of which
Company C was a part, was widely regarded as one of
the best lawmen the state of Texas had ever seen. Cody
had met the major a few times and been very im-
pressed by him. Things must really be desperate if
Jones was asking for help, he thought.

"You want *me* to ride over to San Antonio?" Cody asked. "Seems like the major ought to have plenty of men on hand already."

"Sure he does. But folks over there know most of 'em for Rangers."

Cody began to understand. "Jones wants somebody to work undercover."

"That's right." Vickery shoved back his chair and stood up, his vitality unable to let him remain seated for very long at a time. Pacing back and forth just as he did when he was in the pulpit delivering a sermon, the captain went on, "The major got word that them guns're in San Antone, that whoever stole 'em brought 'em there and is waitin' for the right time to smuggle 'em west to the Comanches. We don't know if they're plannin' to deal directly with the heathens or sell the guns to a band of comancheros. Either way, the Rangers have to put a stop to it. We need to find those guns 'fore they leave San Antone."

Cody nodded. That would solve the problem, all right. He said slowly, "It's been a few years since I spent much time in San Antonio, and the Rangers hadn't been called back into service then. There's a good chance nobody over there knows I'm packing a badge now."

"That's what Major Jones and me are countin' on, son." Vickery clasped his hands together behind his back. "Can you be ready to ride today?"

"Sure." Cody stood up. "I'll start gathering some supplies for the trail. What do I do when I get there?"

"Don't report to the major. In fact, you'd best stay as far away from Ranger headquarters as you can. I'll wire Jones that I'm sendin' somebody, but I won't say who." Vickery consulted the telegram again. "The fella who tipped off the major about this whole business is a saloonkeeper name of Halliday. Runs a place called the Crystal Slipper. I don't know anything about Halliday, so you'd best be careful. Scout around. See if you can come up with the connection 'tween him and them stolen rifles." The captain sighed. "You'll be pretty much on your own, Cody—but I reckon that's what you like, bein' a lone wolf like that."

Cody just smiled. Vickery knew him pretty well. He was already looking forward to this assignment.

He said good-bye to the captain and left headquarters with a wave for Alan Northrup. Supplies wouldn't be a problem; he preferred to travel light and carry only what fit in his saddlebags. His big, rangy lineback dun was in the corral behind the Ranger post and would be happy for the chance to stretch its legs.

Less than an hour later, Cody rode east out of Del Rio past San Felipe Springs, the natural feature that had turned this area into an oasis in the middle of a vast brown landscape. His route would take him almost due east to San Antonio.

Pausing at the top of a small rise, he twisted in the saddle to look back at Del Rio for a moment. Then, with a grin, he took a large gold watch from its special pocket in his jeans and opened it. On its right side was the watch face itself, a very reliable timepiece that rarely gained or lost a second. But it had another use besides telling Cody the hour.

Opposite the watch face was a sepia-toned photographic portrait of a beautiful young girl. Cody didn't know anything about her—no doubt she had been the wife or daughter or sweetheart of the watch's original owner—but he had grown fond of her in a way, without knowing who she was. Rotating the gold frame around the tiny portrait, he freed the photograph so that he could lift it out of the watch. Behind the picture was a shallow space, just big enough for the hand-carved silver Ranger badge that he unpinned from his vest. He slipped the encircled, five-pointed star into its hiding place and replaced the girl's photograph. "Thanks, darlin'," he murmured as he put the watch back in his pocket. Cody then removed his vest and turned the double-sided garment inside out, eliminating any possibility that the telltale holes from the badge's pin might give his identity away.

Precautions completed, he picked up the reins and

urged the dun into an easy, mile-consuming trot toward San Antonio.

Three and a half days of hard riding and long hours in the saddle brought Cody to San Antonio in the middle of the afternoon. He reined in on a hill west of town to look down across the sprawling city. It had grown dramatically in the last ten years or so since the end of the Civil War, and it had hardly been a sleepy little village to start with. He had even heard talk of how the city fathers were pushing for such modern conveniences as streetcars and that newfangled invention just beginning to be used back East, electric lights. Seemed farfetched for such contraptions to exist alongside the ancient Spanish missions that dotted the town, but it was bound to happen sooner or later, Cody thought. There was no holding back progress—or what passed for progress.

He clucked to his horse and sent the dun on into San Antonio, the trail becoming a road—albeit a narrow, crooked one. The afternoon sun was beating down brassily from the blue sky above—by this time of day the clouds that usually drifted in from the Gulf Coast every morning had broken up and blown away—and a hot breeze brought the smell of the city to Cody's nostrils: the delicate fragrance of the flowers grown in gardens around the missions mixed with the odors of cattle, horses, and men.

The long ride had left Cody tired and dusty, and he hadn't bothered to bathe or shave during the trip. He wanted to find a place where he could get a bath—though not a hot one, not on a day like this—and scrape off the whiskers that had sprouted on his chin. Then he'd go look for this mysterious saloonkeeper Halliday.

While riding, he had thought quite a bit about what reason Halliday could've had for getting word to Major Jones about the robbery and the fact that the stolen rifles might be in San Antonio. It was possible Halliday had been in on the plan with whoever had stolen the Winchesters from the supply depot and had been double-crossed by his partners. In such a case a discreet tip to the Rangers might be a way of getting revenge. Could be, too, that Halliday had just stumbled onto the information somehow and had hopes of getting a reward, once the thieves were caught and the rifles recovered. Or there might be some other reason entirely that Cody hadn't thought of. Whatever, he was going to have to play his cards pretty close to the vest and not trust anyone.

Several well-known hotels were located in the main section of town, including an impressive brick structure on the north side of the central plaza, but Cody avoided them. For the time being he wanted to give the impression of being a drifter, so he settled for a smaller hostelry on one of the side streets. Hitching the dun at the long rail in front of the hotel, he tossed his saddlebags over his shoulder and went inside. The dim interior of the lobby wasn't really very cool, but it felt that way to him after being outside.

A clerk who looked more officious than the status of this place appeared to warrant was waiting behind the counter. He looked the tall range rider up and down and said noncommittally, "Is there something we can do for you, sir?"

"Need a room." Cody dug into his pocket and pulled out a coin with the air of a man who didn't have a lot of them to spare. He tossed it on the counter. "That buy one for a few days?"

The clerk picked up the double eagle, looked as though he wanted to bite it to make sure it was real, but refrained and said, "Of course, sir." A little respect was in his voice now, but not much. He turned the register around and plucked a pen from its inkwell. "If you'll just sign in, please. . . ."

Cody scratched *Sam Carson* in the space the clerk indicated. "I'll be wanting a bath, too," the Ranger said. "Been on the trail for quite a spell."

"Certainly. We have the finest tubs in the city. You won't find a better one, even in the Menger Hotel."

"Don't care if it's a horse trough, just so it's got water in it." Cody was being deliberately curt. Until he found out exactly what the situation was, it wouldn't hurt for folks to think of him as some kind of hardcase.

The clerk sniffed and took a key from the rack behind him. "You'll be in room seven. Up the stairs and to your left. I'll have the boys bring up a tub and get started on the water."

"Thanks," Cody grunted, unbending just slightly from his stiff attitude. "Say, you know where I could find a place called the Crystal Slipper? Supposed to be one hell of a saloon."

"I'm afraid I'm not familiar with the establishment, sir," the clerk replied with a shake of his head. "Sorry."

Cody shrugged and headed for the stairs. There'd be plenty of people in town he could ask about the saloon, and somebody was bound to have heard of it.

Since the hotel room was located on the second floor, it caught slightly more breeze than the lobby below it, but the wind was still hot and unpleasantly sticky. The room had a single window with a ledge running underneath, overlooking a narrow alley with another building close by on the opposite side. A bed with a lumpy straw mattress was the main item of furniture. It was joined by a single chair and a small, rickety table. The floor was bare wood, no rug. Cody had seen worse places, but he had also seen a lot better. Still, it suited his purpose.

He tossed the saddlebags on the bed and went to the window. When he leaned over, he could see the bell tower of one of the missions a few blocks away. Although the alley below was deserted at the moment, the sound of traffic from the street in front of the hotel drifted up—the clop of hoofbeats and the creaking of wagon wheels, the occasional shout of anger or amusement from a passerby.

The door opened abruptly behind him, and Cody was turned halfway around, his hand lifting the Colt from its holster, before he had even realized it. He had acted purely on instinct, but he controlled the reaction as he saw the two young, round, frightened faces staring at him over a metal washtub. The boys were Mexican, no more than twelve years old, wearing the usual white shirt, baggy pants, and straw sombreros. Their feet were bare.

Cody let a grin pluck at his mouth as he slid the gun back into the holster. "Sorry, boys," he said. "I should've been expecting you. Bring that tub on in."

They did so, still watching the tall, lean gringo to see whether or not he was crazy or just careful. Evidently they decided that he hadn't lost his mind, because after a moment they returned his grin.

"I am Pedro Herrera, señor," said the bigger of the two youngsters in passable English. "This is my cousin Lupe. Anything you need while you are in San Antonio de Bexar, you ask for us, sí?"

"Sure. You and Lupe going to bring the water up for my bath, Pedro?"

The boy bobbed his head up and down.

"Not too hot," Cody instructed. "I've been riding in the sun all day, and I already feel like I'm halfway boiled."

"Sí, señor, I understand. Texas in the summer is like that."

Pedro wasn't telling him anything he didn't already know. Cody took a couple of small-denomination coins from his pocket and tossed them to the boys, who plucked them deftly from the air. "Skedaddle, now," Cody said, "and fetch that water."

Pedro and Lupe ducked out of the room and headed downstairs. Cody chuckled as he unfastened his gun belt. He had a feeling he had just made two lifelong friends with those coins, and the investment could prove to be worthwhile.

Positioning the room's single chair next to the tub, Cody placed his gun on it within easy reach just as

Pedro and Lupé reappeared lugging large buckets of water. Steam rose as they poured it into the tub, and when Cody frowned, Pedro said quickly, "Do not worry, señor. This water was already heated. We will cool it off with water from the well."

Cody nodded; that made sense. The two boys seemed to know what they were doing, so he kept his mouth shut and let them work. By the time they had added several more bucketfuls of water to the tub, it was still warm but not hot, just the way Cody wanted it.

"Thanks, *muchachos*," he told the youngsters as he began to unbutton his shirt.

"You need anything else, señor?" Pedro asked.

"Don't think so. Thanks anyway."

"A girl, perhaps?"

Cody frowned again. "Don't tell me you've got a virgin sister who's just dying to meet a man like me. I've heard that story before."

"Oh, no, señor, I would not tell such a foolish lie to an hombre like you. My sister is ugly and no virgin. But I know other señoritas . . ."

"No, thanks. You and Lupe run along." The boys looked at each other, shrugged, and turned to leave the room, but Cody stopped them by saying, "There is one more thing you might be able to help me with. Do either of you know a place called the Crystal Slipper?"

Lupe chattered something to Pedro in Spanish, talking so fast that Cody could only follow part of it—enough to know that Lupe was telling his cousin how to find the saloon. Obviously the boy had recognized the name, even in English.

Pedro turned back to Cody. "*Sí*. It is four blocks east of here. Many American vaqueros drink there. Lupe says you will like it."

Cody smiled at the other boy. "*Gracias*."

Lupe looked down at the floor bashfully.

The Ranger waved them out of the room, telling them they could come and retrieve the washtub later. Once they were gone, he finished taking off his clothes and sank down into the warm water. The tub was a little cramped, but he was willing to put up with that in exchange for getting the trail dust off him. He started washing with his left hand, leaving his right free in case he had to snatch up the gun from the nearby chair. Maybe he should have taken Pedro up on the offer of a woman, he thought lazily. Would have made washing his back a mite easier. . . .

Night had fallen by the time Cody rode in search of the Crystal Slipper. Washed and shaved and wearing clean clothes, he crossed the San Antonio River on a narrow, arching stone bridge that was probably over a hundred years old and moved on into the section of town known as La Villita—the Little Village. The way he'd heard the story, the town of San Antonio had been formed from three separate elements: the Catholic mission of San Antonio de Valero, the presidio established by the Spanish military, and the small village populated mostly by Indians that predated both of the others. The city had grown enormously since then, of course, and the original La Villita had become one of its rougher sections, an area of saloons and whorehouses and small, squalid cantinas.

Not that the place didn't have its attractions. The Crystal Slipper, for example, Cody saw as he reined to a stop in front of it, was a large frame building, constructed within the last few years from the looks of it. It had two actual floors, rather than the usual one story with a false front, and a large, garishly painted sign crowned the eaves of the second story. The sign showed a woman's leg, long and shapely and wearing only a thin, lacy stocking. At the end of the leg, a delicate foot was shod in the slipper that gave the saloon its name. Arching over the leg were the words themselves, painted in large red letters: THE CRYSTAL SLIPPER.

A boardwalk ran in front of the building. The double doors in the center were open, the entrance barred only by the usual batwings. Large windows on both sides of the doorway were decorated with fancy gilt scrollwork around the edges, and through the glass Cody could see that the saloon was doing a brisk business. The bar was crowded, and most of the tables were full. Music was coming from a small band ensconced on a raised platform at the far end of the big room, and the dance floor in front of the platform was filled with cowboys and bar girls waltzing clumsily.

Cody grinned as he swung down from the saddle and tied the reins to the hitchrack. The Crystal Slipper reminded him of a lot of other cow-country saloons he had seen, but on a larger, fancier, more cosmopolitan scale. That was typical of San Antonio. He stepped up onto the boardwalk, pushed the batwings aside, and went in.

No one paid any attention to him as he strolled over to the bar. Waiting until a place opened up, he then took his place at the counter, lifting a booted foot to the brass rail at the bottom and placing his left palm on the brightly polished hardwood. He had to wait a couple of minutes until a bartender in white shirt, sleeve garters, and fancy brocade vest came over to him. The man didn't say anything, merely lifting an eyebrow quizzically.

"Beer," Cody told him.

The bartender spoke for the first time. "You got it." He drew the brew from a tap under the bar, filling a glass mug and sliding it across the hardwood to Cody. "Four bits."

That was a bit high for beer, but Cody supposed the extra went to pay for the ornate decorations, like the sparkling chandeliers and the large gilt-framed paintings on the walls. He put coins on the bar, kept his fingers over them until he'd checked the glass, then lifted his hand. The glass was clean and felt cool to the touch, so the beer was cold. The coins disappeared with a deft sweep of the bartender's hand.

Couldn't complain about the beer, Cody thought as he sipped from the glass. The brew was cold, all right, and tasted good. He took another swallow, then set the mug on the counter and leaned forward while the bartender was still within earshot. "Halliday around tonight?" he asked.

"Who wants to know?"

Cody shrugged. "Just a friend of a friend. I was told to look him up."

The bartender smiled faintly, a hint of derision in the expression. Cody suddenly hoped that this man wasn't Halliday himself. He hadn't figured that the owner of the place would be working behind the bar, dressed like the other two bartenders, but it was possible.

"The boss isn't here right now," the bartender said after a few seconds. "Maybe later."

"All right. Thanks."

Cody didn't really believe that Halliday wasn't there. The bartender would probably pass along the message that somebody had been asking about him, and then Halliday would have the chance to look Cody over before revealing his identity. Halliday might not know what to make of him; Captain Vickery had planned to wire Major Jones that a Ranger from Del Rio was on his way to San Antonio, but Cody had no way of knowing if Jones had passed that information along to Halliday. Halliday was bound to be curious about the tall stranger asking for him. Cody mentally shrugged. Let him wonder for a while.

The saloon was noisy and smoky, just like the Rio Grande back in Del Rio. When Cody was halfway finished with his beer, he heard the low murmur that surrounded him change somewhat. A stir went through the room. The Ranger glanced over his shoulder and saw that a beaded curtain leading into a rear chamber had been brushed aside. A woman now stood just inside the room, and evidently it had been her entrance that caused the brief ripple of interest. Cody could understand why. She was as striking a woman as he had seen in quite a while.

She had the beauty that was to be found in many of the girls who worked in places like this, but there was something else about her, something that drew the eye like lodestone drew metal. She was tall and slender, and the low-cut blue dress she wore showed off the creamy swell of high, firm breasts. Her hair was ash blond, worn loose and rather tousled—almost as if she'd just gotten up out of a warm bed. A small beauty mark adorned her right cheek. As she came closer, sauntering along the bar and speaking in a quiet voice to some of the customers who stopped her, Cody saw that her eyes were a deep blue, like a hill-country pond. She turned those eyes toward him as she approached, and their gazes locked for a long moment. She hesitated, then stepped up to him.

"Hello, cowboy. New in town, aren't you?"

Cody's mouth quirked in amusement at the sarcastic delivery she gave the words. Her tone announced that she was no common saloon girl. He'd already gotten that impression from the way the customers refrained from pawing at her as she'd made her way past the bar. She might well be one of the *nymphes de prairie,* as some highfalutin gents were beginning to refer to soiled doves, but she was obviously at the top of the heap here at the Crystal Slipper.

"I'd like to buy you a drink," he said seriously.

"Of course you would. But Angela doesn't drink with just anyone."

He'd seen proof of that. There'd been at least a dozen such offers made as she came across the room, he guessed, and she had politely refused all of them with a laugh and a quiet comment that clearly kept her many admirers from taking offense.

She went on, "What's your name?"

"Sam Carson. And I'm pleased to make your acquaintance, Miss Angela."

"Just Angela, please. Miss is for ladies, and I'm no lady."

Cody might have argued that point. She had a certain class that no amount of paint and spangles could take away. He said, "What about that drink?"

"Maybe later." Her tone sounded just promising

enough to keep him interested. At least she hadn't turned him down flat, the way she had the others.

She gave him another smile and moved on, sort of like a queen surveying her subjects, he thought. He picked up his beer and sipped it again, but he kept his back turned to the bar so that he could watch her directly instead of in the big mirror over the backbar. Nothing unusual about that, he mused. At least half the men in the room were watching her, most of them with the same expression of wistful longing on their faces.

The band had momentarily fallen silent. Angela drifted over to the platform, caught the eye of the leader, and spoke to him when he came over and leaned down to listen to her. The man nodded and went back to the other musicians. He said something to them, and they began playing a tune that was considerably slower than the brassy melodies they'd been playing earlier. Angela swayed back and forth in time to the music.

Cody's breath seemed to catch in his throat. Lord, she did something to a man! Even the simple movements she was making now were enough to keep his eyes fastened on her. If only he weren't on an assignment for the Rangers . . .

But he was, and he forced his mind back to the job at hand. His gaze darted around the room, checking to see if anyone was taking an inordinate interest in him. If anyone was, chances were it would be Halliday. A slight smile tugged at his mouth as he realized nobody was watching him. Everybody was concentrating on Angela.

Her swaying to the music had become more sensuous. She let her head fall back a little, eyes closed, obviously transported by the melancholy tune out of this saloon and into someplace far more private. Cody sighed as he watched her, then downed the rest of his beer.

A young cowboy who had clearly poured a good deal of whiskey down his throat came out of the crowd, reaching for her. Maybe he just wanted to dance with her, or maybe her seductiveness was too much for him. He grabbed her arms and whirled her around to face him.

Cody tensed, expecting trouble. There had to be bouncers stationed around the room, though he hadn't been able to pick them out, and no doubt they would move in within seconds to rescue Angela from the young man's drunken mauling. But instead she made an abrupt gesture with her hand as if to tell any would-be helpers to keep back. She came into the cowboy's embrace, molding her lithe body to his and lifting her face so that he could press his lips to hers in a hungry, demanding kiss. She took hold of his head, making sure he couldn't pull away as her open mouth worked feverishly against his, and ground her pelvis against him.

The kiss seemed to go on forever. Just as Cody began to wonder if the two of them were ever going to come up for air, Angela took her lips away from the cowboy's. The young man's eyes were glassy. When Angela slipped out of his embrace, he tried to take a step after her, but his knees buckled, betraying him and pitching him forward on his face. He didn't move, passed out from the whiskey he had drunk—and maybe from the intensity of Angela's kiss.

A cheer went up from the crowd.

Angela spun around, a bright smile on her face, and reached out to pluck a whiskery old-timer from the onlookers as she signaled the bandleader to play something fast again. They broke into a Virginia reel, and Angela and the old-timer began to kick up their heels.

Cody joined in the laughter and clapping, wondering if the woman put on a show like this every night. She had the place in the palm of her hand, that was for damn sure.

Over the next hour, Angela danced with nearly every man in the Crystal Slipper, picking her partners herself. The other bar girls looked a little jealous, but there was nothing they could do about it. None of them could compete with her, and evidently they were well aware of that fact.

Cody stayed where he was, nursing a second beer. Even though Angela selected men from either side of him to dance with her, she didn't even look at him again. He supposed he should have been slightly offended by that, but his mind was back on his mission again. He'd expected Halliday to make himself known by now. Maybe the man was waiting until later, when the saloon might not be so busy. Cody didn't care for the delay, but he told himself to be patient.

Finally, when it seemed as though Angela had danced with every man in the place except him, she came over to him again. Her exertion had left a fine sheen of perspiration on her face, and her skin glowed pink under the heavy makeup. She smiled up at him and said, "I'll take that drink now."

He started to frame a curt reply but stopped the words in time. He couldn't quite figure this girl out, but she was interesting enough to be worth the price of a drink. Catching the bartender's eye, he crooked a finger and inclined his head toward Angela.

A moment later the bartender set a glass containing a couple of ounces of amber liquid on the bar. The rest of the saloon's customers had gone back to their own drinking, and some of the men were dancing with the other girls. The stairway leading up to the rooms on the second floor was busy as, leading their partners, the girls plied their other trade.

Maybe that was Angela's job here, Cody thought— get the customers so heated up that they'd drink a lot and take the other girls upstairs. If that was it, she was damn good at it.

He glanced at the glass as she picked it up. She obviously saw the look and smiled. "It's the real thing," she assured him. "You're not buying watered-down tea." With a mocking expression in her eyes, she passed the glass closely enough under his nose that he caught the raw scent of whiskey; then she tossed down the liquor in one swallow.

His jaw tightened. "Just what is it you want, ma'am, besides that drink?"

She gave him a long, appraising look, then said, "I want you to come with me. My house is out back."

The answer surprised him. He frowned, but before he could say anything, she went on. "You see, I pick one man every night to accompany me, then I dance with the others. That dance is a bit of consolation, if you will, since that's all they can have of me." She held up a finger and rested it on his lips as he tried to speak again. "Yes, I suppose I am arrogant and sure of myself. But will you be the first one to turn me down?"

Dammit, he didn't want to turn her down. That was the last thing in the world he wanted right now. She *was* too smug, too sure of herself—and he thought he could take her down a peg or two.

But he still hadn't done what he had come here to do.

Stalling, he asked coolly, "Why should you always get what you want?"

She gave him that cocky smile again and said, "Because this is my place. And Angela Halliday *always* gets what she wants."

CHAPTER
||||||||||||||||||||||||||||| 3 |||||||||||||||||||||||||||||

Angela Halliday's house, an adobe building across the alley from the rear of the Crystal Slipper, was a rambling, low-roofed structure surrounding an open courtyard. A wrought-iron gate led into the courtyard from the alley. Looking at the tile-roofed casa in the moonlight, Cody had the feeling it was a lot older than the saloon. In fact, he decided, it had probably been there since the early days of La Villita.

Angela had taken him through the curtained doorway of the saloon into a short corridor that led to a rear door. Cody hadn't known what to expect as they stepped outside; she might've been leading him into some sort of ambush. Even though he hadn't seen the bartender give her any kind of sign that Cody had been asking about someone named Halliday earlier in the evening, that could have happened.

But the night was quiet as they paused in the alley, giving him the chance to study her house. After a moment he asked, "You say you choose a different man to bring here every night?"

She made a face, the prettiness of the pout visible in the silvery light from the moon and stars. "Don't get jealous, Sam. There's no need to be. After all, you're the luckiest man in San Antonio—at least for tonight."

Once she had told him her name, there was no question whether or not he would accompany her. Judging by the looks of envy he had gotten from the other men in the saloon as they left, they knew where he and Angela were going—and why. Evidently she was telling the truth, and it was a common occurrence for her to leave with the one man she hadn't danced with. But as lovely and appealing as she was, Cody had more on his mind than passion. There was also a little matter of two hundred stolen Winchester rifles.

When she took his hand and started toward the wrought-iron gate, he didn't resist, though his mind was going back over the things Captain Vickery had told him while giving him this assignment. Vickery, too, had assumed that Halliday was a man, since the message from Major Jones had just mentioned a saloonkeeper called Halliday. While Angela fit that description just fine, it wouldn't hurt to be careful.

She swung open the gate and stepped into the courtyard with Cody following her. Standing in the center of the patio surrounded by a low wall was a fountain, but it was dry at the moment. Angela led him around it and toward a door on the far side, her hand smooth and cool in his.

When they reached the door, she took a large key from a pocket somewhere in her dress—Cody couldn't have said where; he thought the dress too tight for pockets—and unlocked it. It opened soundlessly on well-oiled hinges. The door was thick, heavy wood, made to withstand attack. The Spaniards who had built this house over a hundred years earlier probably still had had quite a few savage Indians to contend with, and the casas of the early settlers had been constructed accordingly.

Angela reached into a niche in the wall just inside the door and produced a silver candelabra. She lit the three candles with a match—Cody didn't know where she got *that*, either—and then took his hand again, leading him through a foyer into a large room. It was simply but elegantly furnished with a long, heavy-looking wood-framed couch, a couple of chairs, an Indian rug on the floor, and a small table holding an earthen vase full of cut flowers. Cody thought the room had a comfortable look.

Angela placed the candelabra on the table so that the yellow glow from the candles washed over most of the room, leaving only the corners in shadow. She turned to face Cody and said in a soft voice, "Welcome to my home." The smug, mocking tone that had been present in her speech all evening had abruptly disappeared.

He supposed she had to put up a front, a woman alone running a saloon in a place like San Antonio. She had to appear tough and hard-bitten in order to keep people from taking advantage of her.

Her eyes were heavy-lidded with passion as she stepped closer to him. Cody reached for her, and she came into his arms willingly. He kissed her and found her lips parting eagerly. Even through their clothes he could feel her hard nipples as she pressed her breasts against his chest.

Angela Halliday was an armful of woman, that was for damn sure. But, unlikely as it was, she might also be part of the gang that had stolen those Winchesters, the Ranger reminded himself. And despite the need inside him, he didn't intend to bed her until he had found out more about what was going on.

"What's wrong?" she asked in a throaty whisper, evidently sensing the change in him. "I told you, you don't have to be jealous—"

"That's not it," Cody said. He rested his hands on her shoulders and put a few inches between their bodies. "You and I have to talk, Angela."

"Talk?" Her red lips curved in a smile. "Sure, Sam, if that's what you want. We can talk first. But I hope you're not going to disappoint me and make me wish I'd danced with you instead."

She was shamelessly wanton, which was just fine with Cody under normal circumstances—which these most definitely weren't. He let go of her and reached into his pocket. "Something I've got to show you," he said.

"You show me anything you want, cowboy," she said brazenly.

He glanced at her, then looked down at the watch in

his hand. As he flipped it open, her gaze went to the portrait of the beautiful young blond girl inside.

"Oh," Angela said. "You want to show me that picture of your wife. Or is she just your sweetheart? It doesn't matter, Sam. She doesn't ever have to know about tonight."

"She's not my wife or my sweetheart," Cody said. "*This* is what I want to show you."

With a practiced twist of the wrist he removed the picture, and the silver star in a silver circle fell from its hiding place into his open palm.

"Name's really Cody. I'm a Texas Ranger from Del Rio."

His muscles were tense and ready for action as he spoke the words. If this was some kind of a trap—though he couldn't see why she'd have set one for him—he was prepared to move in a hurry and grab her with one hand while he drew his Colt with the other.

But all Angela did was stare wide-eyed at the Ranger badge for a long moment, and then her face hardened into a tight, emotionless mask. She didn't even let out a gasp of surprise.

"Well, I knew you were coming, of course," she said flatly. "Or rather, I knew somebody was coming. You could have told me earlier, before I made a fool of myself."

"Announce I'm a Ranger in the middle of that saloon?" He shook his head. "That would sort of defeat the purpose of me coming here, wouldn't it?"

Angela sighed. "You're right. Of course you couldn't say anything while we were still in the Crystal Slipper. I'm sorry."

"No need for that. Just tell me what's going on around here."

She turned away from him, walking over to stand beside the table. "You know about the rifles?" she asked without looking around at him, toying with one of the flowers in the vase.

"I know about them. Are they still here in San Antonio?"

"I wish I could tell you that. I don't know exactly where they are. I never did."

Cody wanted to believe her. He sensed that she was telling the truth, but he wished he could see her face as she talked to him. The fact that she wouldn't look at him made him suspicious. And her reaction when she saw his Ranger badge was puzzling, too. It was like a wall had come down between them.

"How did you find out about them in the first place?"

Finally she turned and gave him a smile, albeit a weak one compared to the way she had been looking at him earlier. She shrugged. "A woman in my line of work hears things. When men drink too much, they usually start to brag . . . especially when there are pretty girls around. And my girls are some of the prettiest in Texas."

Not to mention the lady in charge, Cody thought. He asked, "So you heard someone in the saloon talking about the robbery?"

"That's right. They were talking about it among themselves at first, but one of the girls overheard them and said something about it to me. I bought them a bottle of champagne to see what I could get out of them."

"Them?" Cody repeated.

"The Grady brothers. Uriah and Calvin. They're . . . hardcases, I suppose you'd say. I don't know everything they've been involved with in the past, but their reputation is certainly on the shady side." Her voice was regaining some of its animation now. She pushed back a lock of the tousled ash-blond hair and went on, "According to rumor, the Gradys have killed several men."

"Rumors aren't always right," Cody pointed out.

"No, but in their case I'd be willing to bet there's some basis in fact."

"How much did you find out when you talked to them?"

She shook her head. "Not as much as I'd hoped to. Liquor loosens tongues, but men like that seem to have some instinct that keeps them from saying too much. All I could get out of them was the fact that they might know something about some stolen army weapons."

"How did you connect that up with a supply depot in East Texas?"

Her smile grew. "The Crystal Slipper doesn't just cater to cowboys and badmen, Mr. . . . Cody, was it?"

"Just make it Cody," he said. "No mister. But to everybody else, I'm still Sam Carson."

She nodded in understanding. "All right. At any rate, as I was saying, my establishment gets its share of army officers, too, when they're off duty. I asked a few pointed questions of the right people and found out that a shipment of rifles had disappeared. That seemed to be the only logical thing the Grady brothers could have been talking about."

Cody had to admit her answers made sense. But she had not yet touched on what might be the most important point of all. He looked at her intently and asked, "Why did you go to the Rangers and tell them about all this?"

For a long moment he thought she wasn't going to answer. That reluctance, along with her instinctive reaction to the sight of his badge, made him even more sure than before that she wasn't telling him everything. At last she said, "I have my reasons. Isn't it enough that I'm trying to be a good citizen and help the authorities?"

The words weren't convincing, though Cody could tell she was trying. "There's more to it than that," he said. "What are you after, Angela?"

She took a step toward him, then another, then suddenly stalked up to him in a rush. Her jaw was taut with anger, making the cords in her throat stand out. She looked older now, and he realized abruptly that she wasn't in her mid-twenties, as he had first thought. She was closer to his own age.

"Damn you, I'm trying to help the Rangers, Cody. Why I'm doing it is my own business. You can either accept that and work with me, or you can get back on your horse and get the hell out of San Antonio!"

He could see the fury in those deep blue eyes and knew that his prodding had shaken her. He didn't trust her, not by a damn sight, but maybe it was time to pull in his horns a little. "Sorry," he murmured. "On behalf of the Rangers, I want you to know we do appreciate your assistance, Miss Halliday." He cocked an eyebrow. "So what happens now?"

She took a deep breath and made a visible effort to regain control of her emotions. "For one thing, you stop calling me miss, as I told you," she said. "Angela or even Halliday will do fine."

"All right . . . Angela."

"That's better. I suppose the next thing is to put you on the trail of the Gradys. If those rifles are still hidden somewhere in San Antonio, those two will know where they are. I'm sure of it."

Cody wasn't sure he shared her certainty. From what he had heard so far, Angela Halliday didn't have any proof of anything. Her story was a mixture of coincidence and conjecture. He was convinced she was telling the truth—as she saw it—but she might be completely wrong about everything.

Still, the only way to determine that was to check things out as far as he could. He asked, "You say these Grady brothers come into your saloon pretty regularly?"

"Nearly every night," Angela replied. "I didn't see them tonight, but they haven't skipped more than one night in a row since they rode into town about two weeks ago. I think it's a safe bet they'll be around tomorrow night. You come to the saloon and I'll point them out to you." Her nearly bare shoulders raised and lowered in a long shrug. "After that it's up to you."

"Fair enough. I reckon that finishes our business for

tonight. Now, about the reason I came over here in the first place . . ." She had backed off a little, so he stepped closer to her.

Her voice was as cold as a Panhandle norther as she snapped, "Like you said, Cody, that finishes our business. Good night."

He inclined his head slightly. Her dismissal didn't take him totally by surprise. Some harsh words had passed between them, and Angela didn't strike him as the type who would be quick to forgive or forget about that. "If that's what you want," he said quietly.

"It is."

He had dropped his hat onto a chair when he came into the room. Now he picked it up and settled it on his head. "If you need to get in touch with me, I'm staying at a hotel called the Carlton a few blocks from here." When there was no response, he added, "Good night."

She had turned around again and didn't say anything as he walked out.

There was no figuring women, he thought as he strode watchfully through the courtyard and then circled the Crystal Slipper to get back to the main street and retrieve his horse. Angela Halliday had presented two or three different faces to him within a short time tonight, and he had no idea which one represented the real woman—if in fact any of them did.

The dun was waiting placidly at the hitchrack. Cody jerked the reins free and mounted, turning the animal back toward the small hotel where he was staying. Despite the late hour a lot of people were on the streets, and he kept his eyes open as he rode. But no one bothered him, and he reached the hotel without trouble.

He was still tired from the long ride from Del Rio, so he dropped onto the lumpy bed almost as soon as he came into the room. Pedro and Lupe had been up to get the washtub, he saw, but other than that, nothing appeared to have been disturbed.

For all his weariness, sleep didn't come right away. Every time he closed his eyes, he saw Angela Halliday's face, and he puzzled over what to make of her.

About all he could say for certain was that he had taken the first step on the job that had brought him to San Antonio.

But it was too soon to tell where that trail was going to lead him.

After eating supper the next night in a little side street *taquería*, Cody was back in the Crystal Slipper. His eyes automatically scanned the room as he pushed the batwings aside and stepped into the saloon. The big, high-ceilinged room was as crowded as it had been the night before, but there was no sign of Angela Halliday.

Maybe not quite as crowded, Cody amended, because he was able to get a place at the bar right away. A different bartender, one he didn't recognize as any of the three men who had been on duty the previous night, came up to him and inquired, "Can I get something for you, mister?"

"Beer," Cody told him. He took out four bits and dropped it on the bar without waiting to be told.

He wondered if Angela made her appearance at the same time every night. The evening before, he had gotten here a little later, so he might have to wait awhile, he told himself. As he looked around the room, his eyes settled momentarily on various rough-looking individuals. For all he knew, he was looking at the Grady brothers.

His impatience grew as he waited for Angela to show up. He told himself not to get edgy. One time out in the Big Bend country, before he'd joined the Rangers, he'd been forced to wait out a band of young Apache braves who wanted his hair. He had been forted up in some rocks with plenty of water, ammunition, and food, so all he had to do was wait and pick them off when they got tired of the game and tried to creep in. It had taken nearly forty-eight hours for that to happen, and he had remained awake and alert the whole time. Surely he could stand to wait thirty minutes for a woman.

Still, he felt a surge of relief when she came through the beaded curtain, making the same sort of entrance as she had the night before. Again everything seemed to stop for a beat as she came in. She wore the same self-assured smile as she made her way along the bar, speaking to customers at random. That was good, Cody thought; she needed to follow her regular routine, just to be sure the Grady brothers didn't sense that anything unusual was going on.

As she got closer, he could see the weariness in her eyes. She hadn't been able to conceal all of it with paint tonight. Maybe her sleep had been as restless as his.

She paused as she reached him, and he wondered if she was planning to pick him out of the crowd again, as she had done the night before. That would be a mistake. She had made it plain that she selected a new man each night to receive her favors. There were enough regular customers in the place who might remember him from the previous night.

But she just smiled, leaned closer to him, and said in a whisper, "Third booth from the back. Now laugh like I said something bawdy, something about last night."

Cody grinned and laughed, giving the bar a slap with his free hand for emphasis. Angela came up on her toes and leaned closer to him, her lips brushing his cheek. Then with a roguish tilt of her eyebrows, she moved on, that devil-may-care smile still on her face.

Smooth, Cody thought in admiration. She couldn't have handled the situation any better. She'd managed to tip him off about the Gradys without anyone in the saloon being the wiser. To a casual observer their brief exchange would have looked as though they were just sharing a ribald memory.

He turned back to the bar with a shake of his head and a rueful smile, as if regretting that he wasn't going to be allowed to repeat last night's events. The man to his right nudged him with an elbow and said, "I can tell what you're thinking, mister. Too bad, ain't it?"

"Yeah," Cody agreed. "Too bad."

"Well, look at it this way: At least you got your memories. Angela's never picked me, and she probably never will. And I been coming in here every night for damn near six months!"

Cody glanced over at him. "But think about how many times you've gotten to dance with her."

"Yeah," the man said wistfully. "There *is* that."

Leaning on the bar, Cody used the big mirror behind the counter to study the room. He focused his attention on the small booths that lined the opposite wall. Sure enough, when he counted three booths from the end, he saw a booth with two men in it, sitting across from each other at the narrow table. With a lot of people moving between him and them, Cody couldn't tell much about them from their reflections in the mirror. He was going to have to get closer.

He drained the beer and motioned for the bartender to bring him another. When he had paid for it, he picked up the mug and sauntered away from the bar, making his way leisurely across the room. He had to dodge bar girls and cowboys and townies and gamblers along the way, and several men stopped him to ask lewd questions about the time he had spent with Angela the night before. For some reason the questions bothered Cody, but he didn't show his annoyance, just grinned meaningfully and moved on.

The booth in front of the one where the Gradys sat was occupied by a burly, bearded man wearing work clothes and shoes. A farmer, Cody decided, who had come to San Antonio for a rare night on the town. The man was drinking heavily and had one of the saloon girls perched on his knee. The heavily rouged and powdered girl was giggling and making a fuss over her companion, and they would probably be heading upstairs before too much longer. Cody hoped so, anyway. He lingered a few minutes, watching a poker game in progress at one of the tables. As far as he could tell, the dealer was on the square, not like Axel Farnum back in Del Rio.

Out of the corner of his eye Cody saw the farmer and

the bar girl leave the booth, and he turned to stroll toward it, still not moving fast enough to draw attention to himself. No one else had claimed the place by the time he reached it, so he was able to slide onto the bench that backed up against the booth where the Gradys were sitting. Taking off his hat, he cocked his booted right foot on his left knee and sat back with the air of a man who was glad for a little momentary peace and quiet. He lifted the beer to his lips and sipped it.

Angela hadn't started the evening's dancing yet. She was still circulating through the room, stopping to talk more often tonight. Maybe she was putting off making a decision, Cody thought.

He wasn't the only one watching her. A moment later he heard a deep voice coming from the booth behind him.

"You think she'll pick me tonight, Uriah?"

A laugh. "Don't reckon I'd hold my breath waitin', was I you, brother. She fancies herself too good for the likes of us." Uriah's voice was more shrill, almost whining.

"Maybe so, but she'll think different when we're rich men." The first man—that would be Calvin Grady, Cody assumed—hesitated, then continued, "She'll sure as hell sing a different tune, once we got that money."

"Sure she will." Uriah didn't sound convinced.

Calvin sighed. "I'd like to touch her. I bet her skin's so smooth. . . ."

The Grady brothers spent the next couple of minutes discussing Angela Halliday's charms. Cody's jaw tightened as he listened, but he forced himself to drink his beer and relax. Angela was nothing to him but a source of information. Hell, hadn't she admitted that she had a different man in her bed every night? Most folks would reckon she was nothing but a slut and a whore.

But he still wished the Gradys would shut up about her.

Finally, Uriah said, "It don't look like she's even

goin' to dance tonight, Calvin. We might as well leave.
I wouldn't mind checkin' on those crates."

"Billy's watchin' 'em," Calvin pointed out.

"I don't care," Uriah snapped. "Sometimes Billy
don't watch close enough. I sure as hell don't want
nothin' goin' wrong when we're this close to leavin'
town."

Cody sat up straighter and leaned his head against
the seat back, edging his ear closer to the corner. Rifles
were carried in crates. And what was that Uriah had
said about leaving San Antonio?

"Reckon you're right." Calvin sighed. "I was sure
hopin' Miss Angela'd pick me one of these nights.
Now there's just one more. If it don't happen tomorrow night, I'll have to wait till we get back to get me a
shot at her."

"You'll survive," Uriah said dryly. "I never heard of
a man dyin' from what you got ailin' you."

"I have! There was a fella in Nacogdoches—"

"Yeah, I heard that story, too, and there ain't a lick
of truth in it. Come on, let's get out of here."

Cody heard them getting to their feet. He picked up
his hat and dropped it on his head, tugging the brim
down to shield his face to a certain extent. As they
walked by, not paying any attention to him, he studied
them as best he could.

Uriah had to be the one in front, the leader in more
ways than one. He had a hawk nose, a long, untidy
mustache, and lank brown hair that fell almost to his
shoulders. Twin cartridge belts encircled his narrow
hips, a heavy Colt suspended on each side. He wore a
brown vest and a shirt that had once been white, and
his battered hat had the brim rolled up on the sides.

Calvin's booming voice would likely belong to the
barrel-chested man following Uriah. He was a few
years younger than his brother, probably not much
more than twenty, but his youth wouldn't make him
any less dangerous. His shoulders were broad and
powerful-looking, and he had long arms that ended in
hamlike hands. A ragged beard extended to his chest.

He wore a brown hat with a low, rounded crown, and a single gun was belted around his thick waist. Cody recognized it as an old Dance Brothers .44 Dragoon.

Neither brother struck Cody as particularly intelligent, but from the way some of the men in the saloon got out of their path, evidently they had a reputation as hombres not to cross. And just because they were involved with the theft of the army rifles, that didn't mean they had planned the job. All that really mattered, the Ranger thought as he finished his second beer and got to his feet, was the possibility that they might lead him to the stolen Winchesters.

The Gradys had reached the doorway by the time Cody stood up. Without hurrying, he followed them. Enough men were coming and going through the batwings that he didn't think he'd be noticed. He saw Uriah and Calvin turn right as they got to the boardwalk outside; when he reached the door, he looked in the same direction.

They had bypassed the horses at the hitchrack, he saw, and were walking along the street about half a block away. From the looks of things they were heading somewhere close enough so that they didn't need to ride their mounts to the Crystal Slipper. Well, there were plenty of cheap hotels in the area. They might even be bunking down in a livery stable somewhere.

Cody cast one last glance into the saloon, trying to find Angela. She was standing all the way at the other end of the room, close to the platform where the band played, and for a moment her eyes met Cody's as he looked back over the batwings. He couldn't read her expression, but after a couple of seconds that seemed longer, she turned sharply away and reached out to snag one of the saloon's patrons. She motioned to the band, and they began to play.

Business as usual in the Crystal Slipper, Cody thought. A muscle twitched in his cheek, and then he turned his gaze back to the Grady brothers.

They were a block down the street now, still heading east. Cody started after them, not wanting them to get

too big a lead. La Villita was busy tonight, the air filled
with guitar music and the laughter of women, and
Cody was hoping his quarry wouldn't spot him among
the other men walking along the street. He kept to
patches of shadow whenever he could.

Uriah and Calvin didn't seem to be in any hurry,
despite what Uriah had said about wanting to check on
some crates—crates containing a couple of hundred rifles, Cody hoped. They ambled along San Antonio's
narrow, twisting avenues, gradually working their way
northeast from the Crystal Slipper. Cody stayed behind them, maintaining a gap of one or two blocks.

Every time the Gradys turned a corner and he lost
sight of them for a moment, he remembered the old
story about how the streets of San Antonio were supposed to have been laid out by a drunken Indian on a
blind mule. That yarn might have some truth to it, he
thought. As the brothers deserted even the side streets
and entered a ratlike warren of alleys and lanes, Cody
closed the distance between them and him. It wouldn't
do to get too far back now. They could enter one of the
adobe buildings that pressed close on both sides and
disappear before he knew where they had gone.

Fewer people were around now in this part of town.
Women called to him from the doorways of some of the
hovels he passed, promising him all sorts of delights in
a crude mixture of English and Spanish. Some of them
even lifted their long skirts to show him, by the light of
candles that sat by the open doors, what he was miss-
ing. A number of men staggered along, most of them
carrying bottles. Several others had already passed
their limit for the evening and were snoring in the middle of the street. Still others who were stone cold sober
waited in the shadows for a likely-looking victim, but
none of them bothered to accost the tall gringo with the
Colt and the Bowie on his hips. They would wait for
easier pickings.

The Gradys vanished around a corner, and Cody
increased his pace slightly, slowing only when he
reached the turn. He took it cautiously, his right hand

close to the butt of his gun. He was fairly sure they hadn't spotted him, but in this part of town, a man never knew what might be waiting for him around a blind corner.

In this case, Cody saw as he muttered a disgusted curse, what was waiting for him was . . . nothing. The Grady brothers had vanished.

CHAPTER 4

Cody's eyes narrowed as he stepped into the alley and searched the gloomy shadows. The far end was blocked by a pile of rubble, and while it was possible that the Gradys might have scrambled over it, he was sure he would have heard the noise caused by that kind of an exit. Several doors in the adobe buildings lined each side of the alley, and Uriah and Calvin could have gone through any one of them.

Loosening the Colt in his holster, Cody walked quietly down the alley. He turned the handle of the first door he came to, but it didn't budge. Barred on the inside, he supposed. The same was true of the others on that side of the narrow walkway. He swung around, prepared to try the ones on the other wall.

A shadow moved between him and the light at the far end of the alley.

Cody tensed as he looked in that direction. Four figures were moving into the mouth of the alley, though from what he could see, none of them were Uriah or Calvin Grady. These men were shorter, more compact. Still, he could feel the menace radiating from them.

"What you doin' back here, gringo?" one of the men called softly. "You lookin' for something?"

"Reckon that's my business," Cody said coolly. He knew them for what they were, thieves and cutthroats who had spotted him venturing into this blind alley. They intended to kill him and steal whatever they could from his body. Out on the street, they might not have jumped him, but they obviously figured that in these close quarters, they could handle him.

"No, señor, it is our business, too," the spokesman said as he and his companions strolled closer. "You should not have come here. You should go back where you came from."

Cody took a step forward, surprising them a little by voluntarily closing the distance between him and them. "Then that's what I'll do."

The leader quickly shook his head and said, "Not without paying first."

A surge of anger went through the tall lawman. The Gradys were probably long gone by now. Either they had spotted him after all, or his luck had simply gone bad. But there had still been a chance he could pick up their trail—until these *charros* had interfered.

"I'm leaving, boys," he said tightly. "Now get the hell out of my way."

A couple of them cursed in Spanish and started forward, lunging at him. Cody drew his gun, but he didn't fire it, not wanting to draw attention. Instead, he lashed out at one of the shadowy attackers. The barrel of the Colt thudded against the skull of the would-be thief, sending him spinning to the filthy floor of the alley. A split second later metal rang on metal when Cody used the gun to block the thrust of the second man's knife. Stepping closer, he slammed a punch into the man's stomach with his free hand, and then he cracked the gun barrel across his attacker's wrist and made him drop the knife.

The other two were now coming at Cody, who grabbed the jacket of the second man and swung him into their path. They stumbled over their crony, one of them losing his balance and dropping to a knee. Cody kicked him in the head and the man sprawled headlong, landing next to his two fallen companions. Cody had disposed of three of them in a matter of seconds, but if the last man felt any hesitation, he didn't show it. He slashed viciously at Cody with the knife in his hand.

Cody was a little off balance himself from the kick and didn't get completely out of the way in time. The tip of the blade ripped through his left sleeve and drew a fiery line down his upper arm. Grunting in pain, Cody pivoted around, thrusting a foot between the man's ankles as the force of his rush carried him on past the Ranger. Cody chopped the gun in his hand against the back of the man's neck. The robber went down and out.

That hadn't taken too long, Cody thought grimly, but long enough. There was no chance in hell that he could find the Gradys again now.

His face set in an angry scowl, he holstered his gun and strode out of the alley, leaving the four men behind him to wake up and lick their wounds. His own injury, the gash on his arm, was burning slightly. As he passed a hovel with a lantern burning outside its door, he pulled back the torn sleeve and studied the wound. It was shallow and didn't look too bad. Hadn't even bled much. He'd go back to the Crystal Slipper and clean it up. He'd planned to go back there anyway, wanting to tell Angela Halliday that their plan had not worked out—at least not yet.

As he closed the distance to the saloon, he wondered if Angela would still be there, or if she had already retired to her house for the evening with whomever she had chosen.

From the conversation that he'd overheard between the Gradys, Calvin planned to be at the saloon one more night before he and his brother left San Antonio. That would give Cody another chance to locate the stolen rifles. The Ranger was convinced that the rifles were still in town but would be shipped out soon. Though the Gradys would be guarding them until they reached their final destination, Cody felt certain that that was the only part the brothers played in the whole affair. Neither of them seemed to be the type to conceive of such a daring scheme, but they would work just fine as hired protection. Hired by whom, was the question that needed answering.

Cody knew he had to make the most of that last chance. Time was running out.

When he reached the Crystal Slipper, a few of the customers gave him curious looks as he made his way to the bar. The torn, bloodstained sleeve of his shirt was responsible for that, he figured. He motioned to the bartender who had brought him his beer earlier.

"What's your name, friend?" Cody asked when the man came up.

"They call me Lew, sir," the bartender replied. He was a competent-looking man, hard-eyed like so many in his line of work.

"Well, Lew, I've got a little scratch here that needs some tending to. Think you can handle it?"

"There are several doctors in town," the man pointed out. "It might be better—"

Cody shook his head. "I don't want a doctor. I want somebody who can keep his mouth shut. Reckon a bartender's about as good at that as anybody I'll find."

A faint smile appeared on Lew's face. "All right. Come on back into the storeroom."

Cody followed him through a door at the end of the bar into a small cubicle where cases of liquor were stacked. Lew brought a partially full bottle of whiskey with him and used it to saturate a cloth. The Ranger pulled his sleeve up and gritted his teeth while the bartender used the whiskey-soaked rag to swab the cut.

"You're lucky," Lew said after a moment. "It's clean and not too deep. Should heal up just fine. Let me get some fresh cloth, and I'll bind it up."

"Sure. Before you go, though . . . where's Angela?"

Lew's voice was flat, emotionless. "She's already retired for the evening."

That was what Cody had figured. But he didn't like the slight bitterness he heard in his tone as he asked, "Who was the lucky man?"

"Nobody," came the surprising answer. "She left early. Said she didn't feel very well."

Cody frowned. He was sorry to hear that Angela felt

poorly, but now he'd be able to let her know what had happened without having to interrupt anything. While Lew was wrapping a makeshift bandage around the Ranger's wounded arm, Cody nodded toward a door on the other side of the storeroom and asked, "Where's that go?"

"Leads to the alley beside the saloon."

"And that goes out back?"

Lew hesitated for a second, then nodded.

"Good. I'll go out that way. No need to go back through the barroom."

Pulling the ends of the cloth into a tight knot, Lew asked, "Mister, just who the hell are you?"

Cody didn't answer right away. He didn't trust Angela, not completely, but he had revealed his status as a Ranger to her. He knew nothing about this man Lew, however. He said, "My name's Carson. Anything else is my business."

"Sure. No offense." The bartender's eyes met Cody's steadily. "But I'm a mite fond of Miss Halliday. I wouldn't want to see her get hurt."

Cody began to understand. Lew was a little in love with Angela, like most of the other men in the Crystal Slipper. Maybe more so, since he worked with her and was around her more than most.

"Don't worry," Cody told him. "I don't want to see her hurt, either."

Lew grunted, and Cody couldn't tell if the man believed him or not. At the moment it really didn't matter. The only important thing was finding those Winchesters before they wound up in the hands of the Comanches.

"That ought to do it," Lew said as he stepped back. "If you're lucky, the wound won't fester. I'd keep an eye on it for a few days, though."

"Sure. Thanks, Lew. I appreciate you going to this much trouble for a stranger."

"*De nada*. Just remember what I said about Miss Halliday."

Cody nodded and went to the alley door. He opened

it and stepped out into the darkness, glancing back for a second before he swung the panel closed. Lew was watching him with a puzzled stare, and Cody knew the man had to wonder what was going on. Maybe when this was all over, one way or the other, Angela could tell him.

Cody turned toward the rear of the building and quickly made his way along the darkened alley. When he reached the back of the Crystal Slipper, he studied the old adobe house where Angela lived. The windows were all dark. Perhaps she really had turned in early. If that was the case, he'd just have to wake her up.

The gate into the courtyard was locked, but that didn't keep him out. Grasping the wrought-iron bars, he lifted himself up and climbed over, a little awkwardly because of his injured arm. When he reached the top, he swung his legs over and dropped lightly to the ground on the other side.

There was a massive brass knocker attached to the heavy door on the other side of the patio. Cody lifted it and rapped sharply, hoping that the sound would be loud enough to wake Angela if she was asleep. He waited a moment, then repeated the knock.

A tiny spy hole set into the door opened. Cody noticed the motion but refrained from bending over and putting his own eye to the hole. He wanted Angela to be able to see who her late-night visitor was.

After a few seconds he heard the door being unbarred on the other side. It swung open, and Angela asked, "Cody, are you all right?"

He heard a note of concern in her voice . . . or at least he wanted to think he did.

"I'm fine," he said as he stepped into the house. "Got a scratch, but it doesn't amount to anything. And it wasn't the Gradys who gave it to me."

"What happened?"

He looked at her. She was wearing a robe with a belt tied around her trim waist, and she carried a candle in one hand and an old Sharps Percussion Revolver in the other, the three-inch barrel pointed toward the floor.

Cody ignored her question and gestured toward the gun. "You know how to use that?"

"You would've found out, if you'd been somebody I didn't want to talk to," she replied tartly. "I've known how to shoot for a long time. Now, are you going to tell me what happened or not?"

Cody gestured with his head toward the parlor where they had talked the night before. "Might as well be comfortable while I'll telling the story," he said.

Angela shrugged and said, "All right. Come on."

She led the way and seated herself on one end of the oak-framed, mission-style sofa after putting the gun down on a table. Cody took the other end of the couch. Before recounting the events since he left the saloon earlier, he studied her for a moment. Her face was devoid of most of the paint she usually wore, which made her true age more apparent but at the same time gave her a more natural, healthy look. Her eyes were alert as she waited for him to begin.

"Hate to admit it, but the Gradys gave me the slip. I don't know if they spotted me trailing them and were trying to lose me, or if it just happened to turn out like that. They went down an alley a few blocks from here in an even worse part of town, and I never saw them after that."

"You didn't try to catch up with them?"

Cody looked down at the bloodstain on his sleeve. "I was going to, but some hombres jumped me. Reckon they planned on robbing me, but it didn't work out that way."

"My God!" Angela exclaimed. "Dead men turn up in those alleys two or three mornings a week. You're lucky you didn't get killed."

"A few risks go with the job," Cody said with a shrug. "Anyway, I overheard the Grady brothers talking before they left, and they're definitely mixed up in something crooked, something they think is going to make them rich. They mentioned some crates they've got hidden somewhere. I'd be willing to bet those crates are full of stolen Winchesters."

Angela nodded. "That makes sense to me. You're going to try to follow them again, aren't you?"

"I'm planning to, but I'll only get one more chance," Cody muttered. "They're leaving San Antonio after tomorrow night. The way I see it, they've got a way of smuggling the rifles out of town, but they've had to wait for something else."

"Do you have any idea what?"

Cody shook his head. "Reckon it'll be plain enough, though, once we find the guns." He stood up. "I'll be back tomorrow night, and we'll try again."

Angela got to her feet quickly as he started toward the door. "Cody, wait!"

He stopped and looked at her in surprise.

"I just meant . . ." Her voice faltered for a moment, then she pointed at his arm. "That wound—you got it fighting those robbers?"

"It's just a scratch, like I told you."

"You should still have somebody look at it—"

"Somebody did," he said. "Your bartender, Lew. Seems like a good man. He cleaned the cut and bandaged it up. I'm sure it'll be as good as new in a few days."

"Oh. Well, that's fine. Lew is good at patching up such things. He's had enough experience, considering some of the brawls that have occurred in the saloon."

Cody delayed his exit long enough to say, "I'm surprised you ever had any brawls. Seems like you run the place smoothly enough to keep any fights from breaking out."

"Now, maybe." Angela grimaced and shook her head. "When I first opened the Crystal Slipper a couple of years ago, it was different. Then, it was a different fight every night—sometimes two or three. I guess some of the customers thought that since a woman was running the place, they could get away with more. It took a while for them to learn that they couldn't. I hired some tough men to work as bouncers and paid them well. Eventually folks learned to behave themselves in my place."

He heard the pride in her voice and knew she had earned the right to feel proud. He said quietly, "Must've been hard, going it alone like that."

Her gaze hardened. "What do you mean by that?" she snapped. "How did you know I was alone?"

Cody shook his head. "Didn't mean any offense. You just talked like you were on your own when you opened the saloon."

"That's right, I was." Angela's tone was still stiff. "But I did just fine, thank you. I don't need anyone's pity or sympathy, and I never have."

Cody held up his hands placatingly. "Whoa! I don't know how that burr got under your saddle, ma'am, but I didn't put it there. If you want, we won't talk about anything but the job that brought me here: finding those rifles."

"I think that would be best." The hardness of Angela's mouth softened a little. "And I also think it would be best if you left now. No one saw you come here, did they?"

"I don't think so." The thought had occurred to him that the Gradys might have spotted him, then taken up his trail in turn after giving him the slip. If that had happened, they were damn good at shadowing, because he hadn't seen them. "But I suppose I'd better go back into the saloon and leave it the way I came in— by the front door—just in case I *was* followed there. Don't want to raise suspicions."

"Make sure no one is watching before you go across the courtyard," Angela said. "We don't want anyone making too much of a connection between us."

"Sure," Cody said, stifling the irritation he felt at the way she was trying to tell him how to do his job. She was just anxious and wanted his mission to succeed, he knew.

As for himself, he wanted to take her into his arms and kiss her. If anything, she was even more appealing without the spangles and heavy makeup. But from the rigid way she was holding herself, he knew that she wouldn't welcome such advances. The lusty side of her nature seemed to have been momentarily sub-merged.

"I know the Gradys now," he said. "You won't have to point them out to me tomorrow night. In fact, it might be better if you laid low. Send word out to the bartenders a bit before the time you usually make your entrance that you're still not feeling well. That way the Gradys might leave earlier and go back to where they've got the guns cached."

Angela frowned slightly. "I don't understand. Why would my not showing up make the Gradys leave?"

"Because I heard Calvin say he's been hoping you'd pick him to come back here with you after the dancing."

A shudder went through her at the thought. "I'll stay away," she said. "Be sure you're there early."

"I'll be there," Cody promised.

He wasn't about to miss what might be his last chance to find those weapons.

As he trotted the dun back through the streets toward his hotel, Cody thought about Angela Halliday. She had altered her routine tonight, claiming that she didn't feel well. But she hadn't seemed ill just now, only a bit drawn and worried. Maybe that was all it was.

But why? Why was she so concerned?

He still didn't know her motive for becoming in-volved in this in the first place. Regardless, she had already done her part to help the Rangers track down the stolen rifles, tipping off Major Jones that the guns might be in San Antonio and pointing out to Cody the men most likely to be involved in such a crime. Most people who had done that much would figure they'd done their good deed, and they'd get back to their own lives. Not Angela Halliday. She seemed to still be as caught up in everything as if she had a personal stake in the outcome.

Maybe she did, Cody mused. He just didn't know what it was yet.

When he reached the hotel, he unsaddled the dun and led it into the small corral out back, then went in the rear door of the building. A couple of small figures were sitting in the hallway just inside, dozing with their backs against the wall. Cody's footfalls woke them, making them look up sharply.

"Señor Carson!" Pedro said. "You need something, yes?"

"I need something, no," Cody replied with a grin. "Just some sleep. It's been a long night."

Lupe exclaimed in Spanish and pointed at the stain on Cody's sleeve, by now dried to a dark brown. Both boys scrambled to their feet, and Pedro stated, "You are hurt!"

The Ranger shook his head. "Nothing to worry about. It's already been tended to."

"But your shirt, it is all torn and bloody. . . . I can get it fixed for you."

He should have seen that coming, Cody thought. "I reckon your mama's a good hand with a needle and thread?"

"No, no. But Lupe's mama is. She can get that blood out and mend the rip so you will never know it was there."

"All right. You come by in the morning and you can get the shirt and take it to your aunt. I'll need it back by tomorrow night, though."

"Oh, sí, you will have it." Both boys grinned broadly as Pedro added, "Thank you, Señor Carson."

Cody nodded, said, *"Buenas noches,"* and continued through the lobby to the stairs. The two boys settled down against the wall again. It wasn't much of a place to sleep, Cody thought, but he supposed it was better than the street.

He moved more quietly as he approached his room, fishing the key out of his vest pocket with his left hand. No point in warning any intruders who might be inside. He stood well to one side as he reached over, slipped the key into the lock, and turned it. Placing his fingertips against the door, he pushed it open.

Nothing happened. The room was quiet.

Cody waited a couple of minutes. Dim light reached the room from the gas lamp on the wall near the landing. The Ranger would be silhouetted against that light as soon as he stepped into the doorway, so he wanted to be as sure as he could that he was entering an empty room.

He heard nothing—no breathing, no soft shuffle of feet or brush of clothing against clothing. Though convinced that no one was lurking inside ready to ambush him, he still went through the door in a rush, crouching low, his gun out.

A man sometimes felt damn foolish acting like this, he thought, especially when it turned out there was no reason for such caution. But he'd rather feel foolish a dozen times a day than let his guard down at the wrong time and wind up dead.

He kicked the door shut with his heel, holstered the Colt, and reached for a match to light the lamp beside the bed. It burned on kerosene, not gas like the lamps in the halls and the lobby. He found the chimney by feel, flicked the tip of the lucifer with his thumbnail, and held the flame to the wick. When it caught, he shook out the match and lowered the chimney. Now he could see good and proper that the room was unoccupied except for him—and a bug or two in the mattress, and he didn't mind sharing that as long as the varmints minded their manners.

He unbuckled the gun belt and hung it on the right-hand bedpost. The bloodstained shirt went on one of the posts at the foot of the bed, where Pedro and Lupe would have no trouble finding it in the morning. Cody sat down long enough to tug off his boots and socks, then stretched out on the bed still wearing his pants and long johns.

The ceiling had cobwebs on it, he noticed as he stared up. The fly-specked view seemed to melt and blur for a few seconds, then coalesce into the face of Angela Halliday. Cody blinked and shook his head, dispelling the vision. In more than thirty years of life

he had known more than his share of women, including
the lovely Marie Jermaine back in Del Rio. There was
no damn reason in the world for him to be so preoc-
cupied with the blond saloonkeeper. He told himself
that she was only on his mind because he wasn't completely sure how she fit into the assignment that had
brought him to San Antonio.

For long minutes he pondered the events of the past
couple of days, until he realized this wasn't getting him
anywhere. With a grunt, he rolled over, leaned out of
the bed, and blew out the lamp. He didn't expect to
sleep very well—again—but at least he could try.
Darkness closed in on the room as he settled his head
back against the pillow.

He wasn't sure how long he had been asleep or even
if he really had been, but suddenly his eyes were open,
searching the room in the faint light that filtered in
through the window, trying to locate the source of the
sound—or whatever it had been—that had roused him.
He couldn't see anything or hear anything now—

A patch of deeper darkness shifted, between him
and the window. Cody hadn't moved so far, lying absolutely still and forcing his breathing to remain calm.
But now he exploded into motion, flinging himself to
the side as he felt as much as heard something coming
through the air toward him.

Cody's hand darted out, guided by instinct. Fingers
closed over the butt of the gun in the holster hanging
on the bedpost. He jerked it free as he rolled away
from the shape looming over him. Someone grunted in
the darkness as the Ranger fell off the bed. A fraction
of a second later he heard the sound of something hitting his pillow—where his head had been resting only
an instant earlier.

He landed on his knees and one hand. The other
hand brought up the Colt, his thumb snapping back the
hammer as the gun rose. He squeezed the trigger and
the revolver boomed and bucked, the roar deafening in
the small room. The orange muzzle flash eerily lit the
darkness for a single beat of time, revealing a shadowy

figure staggering back a step on the other side of the bed. The intruder let out a yell.

Cody fired again, but the man had already spun around and was diving for the window. The Ranger's slug thudded into the wall. As he started to rise, his keen eyes caught a glint of moonlight on metal, and he threw himself back down, sprawling on the floor beside the bed.

A gun blasted twice—loud, jarring explosions that rendered Cody temporarily deaf. He thought the bullets went into the wall above him, but he couldn't be sure. He twisted onto his side, pushed against the planks of the floor with his bare feet, and extended an arm around the foot of the bed, angling the barrel of the Colt up toward the window and triggering another shot. The air in the narrow little room was starting to stink of burned powder.

No more shots came his way, and after a couple of moments his hearing started to return. He heard the clamor of hurrying footfalls over his head.

Hauling himself up, Cody ran to the window and risked a look out. The ambusher was leaving the same way he must have gotten into the room. He had edged along the ledge that ran underneath the window until he reached a spot where he could climb onto the roof of the hotel. Cody could hear him up there, grunting with effort as he scrambled up the slope of the building.

Hoping that there wasn't somebody else covering the window with a rifle, Cody swung a leg out and stepped onto the ledge. It was no more than six inches wide, but that was enough to give him a foothold as he made his way along the outer wall of the hotel. Some twenty feet away was a dormer window, and when he reached the projection, he was able to grasp the top of the dormer and pull himself up.

As the Ranger hauled himself onto the dormer, he looked up and saw a bulky shape vanishing over the top of the hotel. Cody scowled. If he'd reached this position a few seconds earlier, he might have been able to get off a shot. Now there was nothing he could do except start up the roof after the would-be bush-whacker.

His bare feet gave him a slight advantage over the other man, who was probably wearing slick-soled boots and having to go slowly to keep from slipping and falling. Guiding his free hand along on the roof to help his balance, Cody climbed the slope and then went down on his belly when he reached the top, lifting his head just enough to see over.

The intruder had reached the edge of the roof and was looking for a way down. Cody lined the .45 on him and shouted, "Hold it, mister!"

The man whirled around, bringing up his gun. Cody held off as long as he could, wanting to take the ambusher alive, whoever he was. Cody had a good idea of the man's identity, but he wanted to make sure. It didn't look as if he was going to get that chance, though. The gun in the man's hand belched flame and smoke, and the slug kicked up splinters a couple of feet from Cody's head. The Ranger squeezed the trigger.

At the edge of the roof the man disappeared. Cody frowned as he raised up slightly. He would have sworn that the intruder fell *before* he had fired. But that didn't make sense—

Unless the man had simply lost his balance and top-pled off the edge of the roof, unintentionally saving his life in the process. Cody uttered a heartfelt "Damn!" as he heard running footfalls in the alley on the far side of the hotel and realized that was exactly what had happened.

He hurried down the roof, almost falling a couple of times himself. When he reached the edge, he looked back and forth but couldn't see anything in the darkness.

Somebody yelled, "Hey! What the hell's going on up there?"

Cody recognized the voice of the desk clerk. As he looked toward the street, he saw the man peering un-easily around the corner of the building, looking down the alley with the aid of a lantern in his hand. "Bring that light over here!" Cody called.

"What? Who's up there?"

"It's Sam Carson. Somebody just snuck into my room and tried to kill me."

From his vantage point Cody saw someone enter the alley from the other end, from the back side of the hotel. "Señor Carson!" a familiar voice called. "You are all right?"

"Dammit, Pedro, you and Lupe get back inside!" If the bushwhacker was still lurking somewhere around and tried to start the ball rolling again, Cody didn't want the boys getting in the way of a stray bullet. He waited until they had scurried back out of the line of fire, then told the clerk, "Bring the lantern. The shooting's all over."

Tentatively, the man advanced down the alley, holding the lantern high over his head. As the circle of light that it cast reached the point right under Cody's position, the Ranger saw what was left of a rain barrel. Something had landed on it, smashing it to kindling and leaving a huge wet circle in the dust of the alley. A gutter that Cody hadn't seen earlier ran along the edge of the roof. He rotated the cylinder of the Colt to make sure the hammer was resting on an empty chamber, then tucked the gun into the waistband of his pants and grasped the drainpipe. He lowered himself down it just as he had climbed down pecan trees as a boy, then dropped the last couple of feet to the alley.

"My God, it sounded like a stampede up there on the roof!" the hotel clerk said. "And the shooting! If this is the kind of guest you're going to be, Mr. Carson, we may have to ask you to leave."

Cody fastened a hard gaze on him. "I didn't invite that fella to sneak into my room and plant a knife in my pillow."

"A knife!"

"I reckon that's what we'll find when we go up there

and look. Wasn't my idea for the son of a bitch to take some potshots at me, either."

"Well . . . I suppose it does appear you're the victim in all this disturbance. But I'll have to summon the sheriff and let him sort everything out."

Cody shook his head. "No need for that. I'll pay for whatever damages there are. It's plain as day that that bastard just wanted to rob me. He's long gone now, blast the luck."

"But the authorities must be notified—"

"Forget it." Cody's tone was hard, allowing for no argument.

The clerk finally swallowed and nodded. "If you say so, Mr. Carson." It was obvious that the man thought Cody was probably on the dodge himself and that was why he didn't want the sheriff to come. Well, Cody reasoned, the clerk could think whatever he wanted. He himself had more important things to think about.

Like having speculated and then stupidly dismissed as unlikely the notion that the Gradys had spotted him trailing them. It was now all too apparent that they *had* caught sight of him following and then turned the tables—following *him* back to the Crystal Slipper, then here to the hotel. One thing he was fairly certain of, though: They never got close enough to him to get a good look at their pursuer. When Cody had left the saloon, he'd been careful enough to keep his face averted from the light and his hat pulled down, and he was sure no one had come into the hotel lobby behind him, much less followed him up the stairs. No doubt the Gradys—and the Ranger felt sure from the brief glimpses he'd gotten that his attacker was Calvin Grady—had figured out which room was his simply by standing outside and waiting for a light to come on.

He shook his head slowly. The Gradys were craftier than he'd given them credit for.

Then his hands suddenly clenched into fists as a second possible explanation hit him like a blow. There was another way Calvin Grady could have found out where he was staying.

Angela Halliday could have sent him.

CHAPTER
5

Sure enough, there was a long-bladed knife stuck in Cody's pillow, just as he'd assumed there would be. Pulling it loose, he held it out to the hotel clerk, who shrank away and refused to take it.

"Thought you might want it as a souvenir," Cody said dryly. He slid the Colt back into the holster hanging on the bedpost and reached into his pocket for some coins. "Looks like the only real damage is to that feather pillow. You ought to be able to get somebody to sew it up pretty cheap."

"What about the bullet holes in the wall?" the clerk demanded, frowning.

"A little plaster'll fix them right up." He handed over a half eagle. "Five dollars ought to cover everything."

The clerk sniffed, but he took the money. "I'll let you know if this isn't sufficient."

"You do that."

Pedro and Lupe had followed Cody and the clerk up the stairs and were watching with wide eyes from the doorway. Pedro ventured to ask, "Señor Carson, you want to give me your shirt now?"

"Sure. Why not?" Cody plucked the shirt from the other bedpost and tossed it to the boy. "Remember, I want it back by tomorrow night."

"*Sí.*" Pedro hesitated, then said, "Lupe and me, we would be glad to sleep outside your door tonight, Señor Carson, just to make sure nobody else bothers you."

Cody chuckled. "Don't reckon that'll be necessary. You boys go on and get some rest. I don't think anybody else'll come around tonight, not after the reception the last one got."

He hoped that that was true. He had a lot to think about, and he didn't want to be bothered while he was doing it.

After ushering the clerk and the two boys out of the room, Cody extinguished his lamp for the second time that night and stretched his long, lean frame out on the bed. Worry creased his forehead. Ever since he'd realized that Angela Halliday was the only person he'd told where he was staying, a nagging doubt had been gnawing at him.

It was possible everything could have happened the way he'd first conjectured. The Gradys could have turned the tables on him and taken up his trail, following him back to the Crystal Slipper. He had used the side entrance coming and going to Angela's house in back, so if Uriah and Calvin had parked themselves in front of the saloon and waited for him to emerge, they wouldn't know he'd even paid her a visit. Then they could have trailed him back here to the hotel. Cody's eyes were sharp and he stayed alert out of habit, but he knew very well that no man could see everything all the time. He could have missed the fact that he was being followed, especially if the Gradys were good at it.

But he couldn't ignore the possibility that Angela might have told them where to find him. He asked himself why she would do such a thing—and then he was back to why she had gone to Major Jones and gotten involved in this business in the first place. Angela Halliday's true role in this was already a mystery; he couldn't afford to dismiss her as a suspect in the attempt on his life. Sure, if his death was all she wanted, she'd had other opportunities to accomplish that; however, all of them had come on her own territory. She might have wanted to wait until he was well away from the Crystal Slipper before having the Gradys dispose of him.

Cody snorted and rolled over, chiding himself for thinking about Angela as though she were the head of the gang that had stolen the rifles. That wasn't impossible, he supposed, but it was damned unlikely. The Rangers wouldn't have known that the guns were even in San Antonio if not for her. No, for the moment he had to give her the benefit of the doubt—even though it meant admitting that Calvin and Uriah Grady were slicker than he'd given them credit for.

That settled, he tried to go back to sleep. Tomorrow was going to be an important day. By the time it was over, he might have this job wrapped up.

Without knowing where the Gradys were staying, there was nothing Cody could do until nightfall, when he hoped to pick up their trail again at the saloon. He spent the next morning riding around the town, seeing all the ways it had changed since the last time he'd been there. San Antonio still retained a lot of the charm that its Spanish founders had given it, but it was a thoroughly American city by now, too. The two distinct cultures blended easily into a mixture that was very appealing, for the most part.

Cody's home—the ranch that was run by his sisters and their husbands, the place where his mother still lived—was only some forty miles northwest of here, up near Bandera. It would be nice to stop by there and pay a visit when he was finished with this assignment. There had been a time when he had thought often of leaving the Rangers and returning to the ranch to claim his part of it, but more and more now he realized that wasn't likely to happen. He was still devoted to his job as a lawman, and it was looking as though the Rangers might turn out to be his life's work.

Of course, considering the number of owlhoots and renegades he ran up against, that life might not be very long. A man picked his own course and had to live with it, whether it turned out hard or easy.

He thought about that as he rode slowly past the chapel of the mission San Antonio de Valero. Its bullet-pocked walls showed clearly where Crockett and Bowie and Travis and the others had made their stand against Santa Anna forty years earlier. The Alamo, old-timers called it, after the Mexican word for the grove of cottonwoods nearby on the river. At the moment it was being used to store grain, a pretty mundane development considering the events that had taken place there, Cody thought. But then again, the men who had died inside the old adobe walls to help Texas win freedom might not think so. They might be glad that things in these parts had become so peaceful.

Nearby, in an open stretch of ground, he spotted some covered wagons. At least two dozen of the canvas-topped vehicles were parked there, with plenty of folks busily loading supplies and tending to mules and horses and other such chores. A wagon train forming up, Cody mused as he reined in and leaned forward in the saddle, watching. Not as many caravans of that sort made their way across the frontier these days, not with the railroads spreading their steel tracks more and more widely. But pilgrims who couldn't afford to travel by rail still congregated in wagon trains like this one. It was good to see settlers heading west, carrying civilization with them.

If Cody didn't find those guns, things were likely to be a lot harder on those travelers and others like them. A band of Comanches on the warpath and armed with repeating rifles could wipe out even a large wagon train.

After lunch, which he ate at a small restaurant on the central town plaza, Cody went back to his hotel room. The knife-torn pillow had been replaced, and the shirt he'd been wearing the night before was also back, the bloodstain gone and the rip mended so well that he could hardly see it. Pedro hadn't been lying about his aunt's talents with a needle and thread. Cody made a mental note to give the two boys another couple of coins when he saw them next. He stretched out on the bed to try to get some rest. His left arm was a little stiff and sore from the knife wound, but it didn't seem to be infected.

Time dragged as Cody dozed. He skipped supper, not being in the mood to eat again, and finally it was late enough to head back to the Crystal Slipper.

When he got there, the man called Lew was on duty behind the bar, along with two other men. Cody and the bartender exchanged curt nods. Lew wouldn't know the details, of course, but he was sharp enough to be aware that *something* was going on. Cody wondered just how far he could count on the bartender's help in case of trouble. That would depend on how deeply Angela was involved, he supposed.

Cody picked up a beer at the bar and then sauntered over to one of the vacant booths. Though fairly confident that the Gradys wouldn't be able to pick him out, he chose the darkest booth he could find. He'd gotten here earlier than on either of the previous two nights, so the Crystal Slipper, while doing a brisk business, wasn't as busy as it had been. That would change over the course of the evening, Cody was sure—at least until it became known that Angela wouldn't be putting in an appearance this night.

The Ranger hunched down and nursed his beer, keeping an eye on the batwings. Sweat beaded on his forehead under the brim of his hat. All day long, the air had been hot and sultry, and dusk hadn't brought any cooling with it. The air still felt heavy. It was liable to rain later, though the clouds might just tease the thirsty ground below and give up only a few widely scattered drops of moisture.

Cody tilted his hat brim lower over his eyes and listened to the chatter around him as he watched the door. The band wasn't playing yet, so there was no music other than the rattle of poker chips, the clink of glasses, and the bright, artificial laughter of the bar

girls. Cody felt his nerves growing tighter the longer he
waited. The Grady brothers still hadn't shown up.

He wasn't the only one getting fidgety. He overheard
several men asking each other when Angela was going
to come in. No one seemed to know. When a few of the
customers put the question to Lew, the bartender just
shrugged and shook his head.

Cody eased his watch out of his pocket and opened
it. A few minutes after ten o'clock. The Gradys should
have been here by now, and it was past time for Angela
to put in an appearance, too.

The door leading to the storeroom, and therefore the
alley, opened, and a small woman in a plain blouse,
skirt, and shawl came hurrying into the saloon. She
went straight to the bar and spoke to Lew in a low
voice. The woman was Mexican, Cody saw, probably
one of Angela's servants, none of whom he'd encoun-
tered so far. Lew nodded, looking faintly upset. That
confirmed Cody's guess. The woman had just passed
along the news that Angela was still under the weather
and would not be appearing tonight.

Cody grimaced. The Gradys were supposed to have
already been here when that word came. This was just
a minor hitch, though, he told himself. The plan could
still work.

Movement at the door caught his eye, and he turned
his attention back there. Uriah Grady had just shoved
through the batwings, and Calvin was entering behind
him. Cody's pulse sped up a little when he spotted the
sling that Calvin was wearing to support his left arm.
The lawman had been fairly certain that he'd winged
his bushwhacker the night before, and now he was sure
of it, for he'd also been sure that Calvin Grady was the
intruder.

Uriah and Calvin walked over to the bar, and again
Cody noticed how men got out of their way. The brothers bellied up to the hardwood in a just-vacated spot
and ordered drinks from one of the other bartenders,
not Lew. As the white-aproned man poured their whiskey, Uriah asked him a question. Cody couldn't hear

the words over the noise of the saloon, but he could make a good guess that Uriah was asking where Angela was. From the disgusted looks on the faces of both brothers when the bartender shook his head and spoke briefly, Cody knew he was right.

He was watching them in the mirror behind the bar. So far, they hadn't even glanced in his direction. Calvin picked up his drink, tossed it back, then wiped the back of his mouth with his sleeve. Uriah downed his whiskey more slowly, but he was finished in a moment. Clunking the empty glass down firmly on the bar, he tossed a coin after it and then turned away with a scowl on his face. Calvin followed him as he stalked to the door and slapped the batwings out of the way.

This was going to be tricky, Cody thought as he got to his feet. The Gradys knew who he was, and it would be harder to follow them without being spotted. He gave them a minute after they left the saloon, then went to the door of the storeroom. Lew frowned curiously when he saw Cody departing by that route, but the bartender didn't challenge him.

Cody had his hand on the butt of his gun as he stepped out into the alley. Nobody was waiting for him. Striding rapidly toward the street, he peered around the corner of the building when he reached it. Uriah and Calvin Grady were a block away, moving fairly slowly and heading in the same direction they had taken the night before.

The Ranger looked up and down the street and noticed a Mexican leading a burro along the narrow thoroughfare, heading in the opposite direction from the Gradys. Cody lifted a hand as he emerged from the alley and called softly, "Wait a minute, old-timer."

The Mexican, who had a white beard and a seamed face the color of saddle leather, looked at Cody expressionlessly, waiting to see what this tall gringo wanted. Cody held out a double eagle toward him and said in Spanish, "I'd like to borrow that burro from you."

"For that much money, you could buy a burro, señor," the old man replied in English.

"True, but I want the loan of your sombrero and your serape, too," Cody explained, glancing down the street. The Gradys were still in sight, but they were building a considerable lead.

The Mexican nodded shrewdly. "I understand, señor. You wish not to be noticed. I must warn you, though, you are very tall to pretend to be one of my race."

"Reckon I can slouch a mite," Cody said with a forced grin. "How about it, old-timer?"

"Sí." The man took off his straw sombrero, which had an even taller crown and wider brim than Cody's headgear, and handed it to the Ranger. The serape followed. At one time, the woolen cape had had designs woven into it, but time and use had faded it to an almost uniform brown.

Cody lifted the serape and let it settle around his shoulders. It was hot, especially on a muggy night like this, but he thought he could stand it for a while. As he placed the sombrero on his head, he said to the Mexican, "If you'll wait right here, I'll bring your gear and the burro back as soon as I can."

"Sí, señor. I will be here."

Holding up a finger, Cody stepped to his dun, which was tied up at the hitchrack. Hanging his hat on the saddle horn, the Ranger stowed his silver spurs in the saddlebag, patted the animal on the shoulder, and then turned back to the old man and took the burro's lead rope from him. He started down the street after the Gradys, letting his shoulders slump so that he would look a little smaller and keeping his head down as much as possible so that the sombrero would shield his face to a certain extent.

The transaction with the elderly Mexican had been accomplished in the shadows along the boardwalk, and it was doubtful the Gradys would have been able to see what he was doing even if they had looked back. Finding such a disguise close at hand had been a stroke of luck, Cody knew, and he didn't want to waste it. He led the burro as fast as he could without looking conspicuous, trying to cut down on the lead that the hardcase brothers had built. He had almost delayed too long, he saw. Uriah and Calvin were just turning a corner up ahead. Another few moments and they would've been out of sight without him knowing where they'd gone.

The route they followed was familiar, Cody realized as he trailed them. They were going the same way they'd gone the night before, through the roughest section of town. No one bothered them; evidently the thieves who frequented this area knew the brothers' reputation and had decided to leave them alone. Cody didn't draw any attention, either, as he stayed about a block behind the Gradys. The old serape, the battered sombrero, and his bent stance made him appear to be old and harmless and, more importantly, poor. The local thugs wouldn't think he was worth bothering with.

As Uriah and Calvin drew nearer to the alley where they had disappeared the night before, Cody closed in on them even more. He didn't want to lose them again, not when this was his last chance to find out where those mysterious crates of theirs were hidden. But the Gradys walked right past the alley tonight, heading on down the street and soon coming to the San Antonio River. They crossed the winding stream on a wooden footbridge and kept heading east.

There was less traffic on the streets on this side of the river, and Cody knew he was going to be more noticeable as he followed the Grady brothers. That couldn't be helped. He dropped back a bit as Uriah and Calvin strode on toward the Alamo, just up ahead on the left.

Suddenly, two men stepped out of the mouth of an alley between Cody and the men he was following. The Ranger tensed. They were Americans, he saw by the faint light coming from an inn across the street. Both wore range clothes and had pistols on their hips. One of them stuck a quirly in his mouth as they strode into Cody's path and said, "Hey, *viejo,* you got a light?"

"No, señor," Cody mumbled, keeping his eyes downcast as he shook his head.

"You sure about that?" the man snapped.

"Oh, *sí, señor*."

The second man said, "Come on, Fred. This is just an old Mex. He ain't the one we're lookin' for."

Fred shifted the quirly to the other side of his mouth. "Reckon you're right. Let's step back—"

Cody had started moving on when the man's voice abruptly broke off in midsentence. The two of them had to be working with the Gradys, he figured, and were waiting to ambush anybody who was following Uriah and Calvin. That guess was confirmed when the one called Fred declared to his crony, "Stop that old man, Billy. There's somethin' about him I don't like."

The Gradys had referred to someone named Billy the night before, Cody remembered, and now here he was in person. Billy reached out and grasped Cody's arm, jerking him to a halt. "Hold on there, mister," he ordered. "We want to palaver with you some more."

Cody cast a glance toward the Gradys, who were still walking. They were cutting through the courtyard in front of the Alamo now. Putting a whining tone in his voice, Cody said, "*Por favor, señores,* I am just a poor old man—"

Fred reached for the brim of the big sombrero. "The hell you are," he muttered. "Let's just have a look at you." He jerked the sombrero off Cody's head and tossed it aside.

Cody was already moving before the hat hit the ground. His left hand grabbed the bottom of the serape and threw it up over his right shoulder, putting the Colt in the clear; his right hand closed around the walnut butt and lifted the gun smoothly from the holster. As Cody cleared leather, Billy yelled, "It's him!" Both of the hardcases reached for their own guns.

They were too slow. Cody squeezed the trigger, then fanned the hammer with his other hand. The Colt boomed twice, the shots coming so close together they almost sounded like one. Billy was thrown backward as the slugs drove into his body. Cody pivoted slightly to bring the barrel to bear on Fred. The gun roared again.

Fred got one shot off, but it went into the ground at his feet as Cody's bullet slammed into him. He reeled away, lost his balance, and went down hard.

Cody spun back toward the Gradys.

The sudden burst of gunfire had made them whirl around. Uriah already had a revolver in his hand, and Calvin was pulling his own gun from its holster. "Goddamn!" Uriah yelped. "He shot Fred and Billy! Kill him!"

Almost a hundred yards separated Cody from the brothers, too far for a pistol to be accurate. That didn't stop Uriah and Calvin from blazing away at him. Cody ducked into the alley where Fred and Billy had been waiting. That was the nearest cover. Pulling the serape up and over his head, he dropped it on the ground so that it wouldn't interfere with his movements. He thought about the Winchester resting snugly in its saddle boot, back on the dun tied in front of the Crystal Slipper, and he mouthed a heartfelt curse. If he'd had the rifle, he might have been able to do some damage. As it was, he was going to have to get closer to the Gradys before he'd even have a chance to put up a fight.

The brothers had stopped firing by now, realizing that they were wasting cartridges. As Cody stood with his back against the wall of a building, he heard Uriah call, "Circle around! Don't let him get away, Calvin!"

Calvin's voice was farther away as he replied, "I won't! He did for Fred and Billy, and he's got to pay!"

Cody moved along the wall toward the rear of the alley. He couldn't let them pin him down here. The game was out in the open now, but he still had to accomplish the goal he'd started out with: finding those stolen rifles.

There was no question in his mind that the Gradys had been setting a trap for him tonight. The brief conversation between their two henchmen had been

enough to confirm that. Uriah and Calvin had fully expected to be followed when they left the Crystal Slipper, leaving Fred and Billy to intercept anyone who
trailed them. And Cody had played into their hands; he
hadn't had any other choice.

The Ranger had almost reached the other end of the
alley when he saw movement from the street. A figure
staggered into view and lifted a gun. "He went down
here!" the man bellowed in a choked voice, and even
though Cody had heard him say only a few words earlier, he recognized the voice as belonging to Fred. The
bullet he'd taken hadn't killed him after all, but from
the way he was moving, he was badly hurt. The hardcase started down the alley toward Cody, trying to
raise his gun enough to fire it.

Cody said, "Damn," and squeezed off a shot. Fred's
head snapped back and he folded to the ground, the
limpness of his limbs testifying that he was dead this
time. Cody didn't waste any time checking. He darted
around the corner and ran along the rear wall of the
building.

A pistol roared from a spot several buildings away.
Cody heard the slug whine over his head. He had only
one bullet left in the chamber of his own gun, so he
didn't return the fire. Instead, he ran into another alley
and crouched beside a rain barrel. Thumbing out the
empty shells, he loaded fresh ones, slipping cartridges
into all six chambers this time.

He heard Calvin Grady coming along the rear of the
buildings. The big man was trying to move quietly, but
he was too awkward to achieve much stealth. Calvin
was breathing hard, too, and Cody could hear those
rasping breaths as well. But where was Uriah? He
couldn't concentrate so much on Calvin that he let the
elder brother catfoot up and surprise him.

It'd be best if he could take both of them alive, but
failing that, he wanted Uriah as his prisoner. The
Ranger doubted that Calvin actually knew all that
much about the scheme he was involved in, but Uriah
would be aware of what was going on. Cody wanted

more than just to recover the army's Winchesters. He wanted the man behind their theft.

Cody moved in silence toward the street that ran in front of the Alamo, and as he edged forward, he saw that the street and the plaza in front of the old chapel were deserted. Anyone who had been there had apparently, wisely, cleared out in a hurry when the shooting started, and Cody was relieved, because he wouldn't have to worry about an innocent bystander getting in the way of a bullet. Nobody was skulking around right now except him and the Gradys.

He crouched at the corner of a building and studied the open space before him. A wagon was parked in front of the building, but that was the only cover for fifty yards. The doors of the chapel were open, but he'd never reach them if he started across the plaza. There was no sign of Uriah or Calvin. It was possible that Calvin had missed the alley the Ranger was in and was still wandering around back there behind this block of buildings.

As Cody waited in the darkness he heard the faint rumble of distant thunder and saw a flickering in the heavens over the high, scroll-topped pediment of the chapel. One of the evening thunderstorms so common this time of year was on the move. A gust of fresh, cool air bearing the scent of rain blew through the plaza. Lightning danced across the sky again, and a moment later, Cody felt one of the first drops strike the back of his hand. More raindrops fell in the plaza, widely spaced and creating little craters in the dust.

The scrape of a boot behind him made Cody throw himself forward, dropping to the ground as a gun exploded. Rolling to one side, he brought up his Colt, spotting the dark figure running through the shadows toward him. From the size of the attacker he figured it had to be Calvin Grady. A second later, Calvin shouted, "I got him, Uriah! I got the son of a bitch!" He started to squeeze off another shot just to make sure.

Cody fired first, aiming low. Calvin let out a shriek of

pain and spilled off his feet, landing so hard that the ground seemed to shake from the impact. The Ranger scrambled to his feet. He could tell from Calvin's high, keening screams that the man was hurt badly and was probably out of the fight. That left Uriah to deal with.

A shot came from Cody's right. He felt as much as heard the bullet whip past his face. Jerking his head around, he saw Uriah dart out from another alley and start down the street toward him, firing as he came. Cody snapped a shot toward him and then flung himself behind the parked wagon.

In the alley Calvin's shrieking abruptly fell silent, and the quiet was more disturbing than his cries.

"You bastard!" Uriah shouted. "You killed my brother!"

That hadn't been Cody's intention—he had shot low in hopes of simply wounding Calvin and removing him as a threat—but it was possible the younger Grady brother had been mortally injured. Cody frowned as he knelt behind the wagon. From the sound of Uriah's voice, he had taken cover close by, and they were facing a standoff.

"Give it up, Grady!" Cody shouted. "You're not going to get away!"

"I don't want to get away, mister! All I want is to kill you!" A cackling laugh sounded, and Cody thought it sounded a bit insane. "I don't know why you been nosin' around in our business, but it don't matter. You shot my brother, and you're goin' to pay!"

Cody thought about darting out from behind the wagon and trading shots with Uriah, but he wasn't sure where the man was. Uriah probably had him pinpointed, and the second Cody showed his face, the hardcase would be ready to gun him down. On the other hand, if Cody kept waiting him out, Uriah would have to make a move sooner or later.

That move came sooner than Cody expected. Suddenly he heard glass shatter and smelled an unmistakable odor—the sharp bite of kerosene. It was close by, too. He realized that Uriah had thrown a lantern into the bed of the wagon he was using for cover.

Cody looked up at the sky. The rain, which hadn't amounted to more than a few drops, had stopped completely now. The Ranger bit back a curse. He could have used a good downpour right about now—and for more reasons than just to break the drought that gripped the area.

He heard the rasp of a match being struck and knew he had to move. As he dove away from the wagon he saw out of the corner of his eye the streak of fire in the night as Uriah threw the match into the wagon from a recessed doorway some ten feet away.

The spilled kerosene went up with a *whoosh* of flame, the blaze engulfing the wagon in a matter of seconds. Uriah Grady followed the match out the doorway. Cody was rolling in the other direction, toward the plaza in front of the Alamo. He came up on his knees as Uriah fired blindly into the mass of flames that had been the wagon.

"Grady!" Cody shouted as he leveled his Colt. He still wanted to give Uriah a chance to surrender.

Uriah wasn't having any of it. He whipped around toward Cody and fired again, the slug plowing a furrow in the dust a foot to the Ranger's left. Instinctively, Cody squeezed the trigger and let the hammer fall. Thunder from the receding storm blended with the roar of gunfire.

Uriah jerked back as Cody's slug punched into his chest. The owlhoot hit the wall of the building, bounced off, and staggered forward a couple of steps. Shakily, he lifted his gun to fire again. But Cody, hoping that the first bullet hadn't inflicted a fatal wound, put another slug through Uriah's left leg. Uriah spun to the ground, his gun slipping from his fingers.

Cody stood up and darted over to the fallen hardcase. He kicked Uriah's gun out of the man's reach, then knelt beside him. By the sporadic illumination of the lightning and the burning wagon Cody could see

the large dark stain on Uriah's shirt. He could tell from
the sound of the man's labored breathing that he'd
been shot through the lungs.

"Listen to me, Grady!" Cody said urgently as he
lifted Uriah's head. "I'll get you a doctor, but first
you've got to tell me where those rifles are."

Uriah's eyes fluttered open. "D-doctor?" he repeated. "No sawbones . . . is goin' to do me any
good."

Cody's jaw tightened. He'd determined that the man
was hurt too badly to make it, but he'd hoped that
Uriah didn't realize that.

"Those Winchesters can't mean anything to you
now," the Ranger said, his voice grim as he took another tack. "Why don't you tell me where they are so
that I can stop them from killing a lot of your fellow
Texans?"

Uriah gasped for breath until he had enough air in
him to answer, "I don't . . . give a damn . . . about
Texans. I'm from . . . Arkansas!" A spasm of coughing
shook him, and blood spattered from his mouth. When
the coughing passed, he blinked up at Cody and asked,
"Who . . . who the hell are you, anyway?"

It wouldn't do any harm to reveal his identity now,
Cody thought. In a low voice he replied, "I'm a Texas
Ranger."

"Well, you can . . . go to hell, Ranger. Don't know
how you found out about them repeatin' rifles"—Uriah
seemed to strengthen for a moment, and the hate came
through clearly in his voice as he went on—"but you'll
never find 'em, you bastard! The creeks'll run red with
blood . . . once the Comanches get their hands . . . on
them Win—"

His head dropped limply to the side.

Cody let go of the dead man and stood up. Instinct
had guided his first shot at Uriah, and this was one of
the rare occasions when that instinct—and his aim—
had been too good.

Maybe there was a chance Calvin was still alive. He
might have passed out from the shock of his wound.

Cody turned and stalked past the wagon, which had burned down to nothing but a heap of glowing embers. Luckily the fire hadn't spread. Since the wagon had been surrounded by the dirt of the plaza, the flames had been confined to the vehicle alone.

Cody kept his gun out and ready as he walked into the alley to where Calvin lay on his back. With his free hand he fished a lucifer out of his pocket and struck it on the wall of the building. One look at Calvin's glassy eyes staring up sightlessly at him was enough to tell the Ranger that his luck was still running bad. The hastily aimed bullet had caught Calvin in the inner thigh, knocking him off his feet and tearing through the big veins and arteries there. Blood had formed a dark pool underneath him, puddling as it drained out and took Calvin Grady's life with it.

Sliding his gun back into its holster, Cody shook the match out and dropped it, then turned and walked out of the alley. Now that the shooting had been over for a few minutes, signs of life began to reappear in the surrounding blocks. Men poked their heads out of doorways and looked to see if the trouble was over. Someone shouted that he was going for the sheriff. Cody looked across the plaza, past the impressive façade of the Alamo, and saw torches and lanterns moving around in the encampment where the wagon train was forming. People would be coming to investigate not only the shooting but also the fire that had destroyed the wagon.

The Ranger drew a deep breath and let it out in a ragged sigh. The Gradys and their two confederates were all dead—and with them had died the knowledge of the place where the stolen rifles were cached. None of the dead men had known that he was a Ranger, only that he'd been following them and poking into their affairs. But that didn't particularly help Cody now. He felt sure there were more members of the gang in San Antonio and that they'd continue with their plan to smuggle the guns farther west to the Comanches. With

his leads dead, Cody thought that finding the
Winchesters was going to be next to impossible.

Unless . . .

A few final, belated drops of rain pattered down, and
then they too were gone. And so was Cody.

CHAPTER
6

The old Mexican was waiting on the boardwalk in front of the Crystal Slipper, sitting with his knees drawn up and his back against the wall. His face wore a placid expression as Cody trudged up leading the burro and carrying the old man's sombrero and serape.

"Thanks, old-timer," Cody said as he held out the gear. "The serape got a little dirty, but I brushed it off as best I could."

The Mexican got slowly to his feet and took his things. "You found what you were looking for?" he asked.

Cody shrugged. "Maybe yes, maybe no. Reckon you were beginning to worry about whether or not I was coming back with your burro and your belongings."

"No, señor, I was not concerned. You said you would be back, and I trust you. You are a man of honor."

"How the devil would you know something like that?" Cody asked, frowning. "You never saw me before tonight."

The Mexican smiled, exposing dark, stubby teeth. "I am an old man. I have learned to recognize who I can trust and who I cannot. That is how I have been able to live all these years."

Cody understood what the man was saying. He returned the smile and said, "Well, thanks again." He lifted a hand in farewell as the old-timer shrugged into the serape, settled the hat on his head, and led the

burro away, going back to whatever errand had occupied him earlier.

Cody got his hat and spurs off the dun, then looked
at the Crystal Slipper. He could see through the big
windows that the saloon was still busy. A part of him
wanted to go in there and down a good stiff drink. He
had been too close to death more than once tonight,
and cashing in his chips in some filthy San Antonio
back alley wasn't the way he wanted to go.

But other things were occupying his mind as well, so
he decided not to venture into the saloon right now.
Instead, once he had the silver spurs fastened on his
boots and his hat sitting on his head, he went down the
alleyway beside the building and came out in the narrow lane in front of Angela Halliday's house.

The wrought-iron gate was locked, as usual, but that
didn't stop him any more than it had the last time.
Climbing over the gate, he strode across the courtyard,
skirting the fountain, to the door and gave the knocker
a couple of sharp raps, then waited. Within minutes the
door opened, and the servant woman he had seen earlier inside the saloon peered out at him.

"Tell Señorita Halliday that Sam Carson is here to
see her," he said when the servant woman just stood
there silently.

"She is ill," the woman said curtly.

"Tell her anyway," Cody snapped. He was in no
mood for delays. With the Grady brothers dead he was
going to have to play a hunch and check out the idea
that had occurred to him after the gunfight near the
Alamo, but he wanted to talk over his hastily formed
plan with Angela.

The woman shrugged and retreated into the house
again, closing the door in his face. Cody waited impa-
tiently for several minutes until the servant reopened
the door. Her attitude was different now. "She will see
you," the woman said respectfully.

Cody followed her through the door and into the parlor where he and Angela had talked before. The saloonkeeper was standing in the middle of the room, the

silk dressing gown she wore flowing over her curves.
Damn, she's one hell of a woman, Cody thought, trying to get his mind back on why he had come.

Her blue eyes fastened intently on Cody's face as
she asked, "What happened?"

Cody glanced at the servant, who hastily left the
room through another door, shutting it behind her.
Cody took his hat off and moved closer to Angela.
"The Gradys are dead," he said in a quiet voice.
"They set a trap for me. I had to kill them and the two
men who were working with them."

Her eyes widened in surprise. "They knew who you
were?"

Shaking his head, Cody said, "No, I'm pretty sure
they didn't. All they knew was that I'd been following
them. In fact, this was their second try for me."
Quickly, he told her about Calvin Grady's attempt on
his life at the hotel the night before.

Angela's face paled a little as he described that scene
and then told her about the showdown he'd had with
Uriah and Calvin and the other two men less than an
hour ago. Cody watched her closely as he spoke, and
he decided that either she hadn't known anything
about the incidents or she was one hell of an actress.

When he finished, she asked, "You didn't have a
chance to find out where the guns are hidden?"

"I asked Uriah Grady before he died." Cody smiled
sardonically. "He told me to go to hell."

Angela sighed and looked almost as if she wanted to
cry. "Then we've lost," she said. "There's no way to
find the rifles now." Her hands clenched into fists, so
tightly that her long fingernails had to be digging painfully into her palms. "The Indians will get them after
all."

"Maybe not," Cody said. "I've got an idea. . . ."

She frowned and looked at him expectantly.

"Both nights when I followed the Gradys, they were
headed in the general vicinity of the Alamo. Tonight, in
fact, they went right to it. You know anything about the
place?"

"Just what everybody else knows," Angela replied.
"I've heard stories about the battle against Santa
Anna's army all my life, but that's all."

"The old chapel's used for storage now, mostly for
sacks of grain. But other things could be kept there,
too."

Angela's eyes widened. "The crates of rifles!" she
exclaimed.

"That's my hunch, anyway. The building's never
locked up, as far as I know, so the Gradys and the other
folks in the gang could've gotten in and out anytime
they wanted. And if they covered up the crates with
sacks of grain, it's not likely anybody'd have noticed
them."

"That makes sense. Did you search there tonight?"

Cody shook his head. "Nope. That plaza was fixing
to get too busy. Four dead men were lying around, and
I didn't feel like trying to explain everything to the
Bexar County sheriff. A wagon train's forming up
nearby, and all those folks were about to come over to
take a look at things, too."

"We could go back and search the Alamo after everything has calmed down, then," Angela suggested.

"*I* could. You've done your part already, and more
besides. But there's something I want to know first
about that wagon train. Have you heard much talk
about it?"

Angela looked confused. "A little. What does a
wagon train have to do with those stolen Winchesters?"

Cody ignored her question and asked another of his
own. "Do you know when they're planning to pull
out?"

"The settlers? Tomorrow, I think. Or maybe I should
say later today. It's after midnight."

Cody's mouth tightened. "I was afraid you'd say
that, considering what Uriah and Calvin said about
leaving after tonight. There's not much point in searching the Alamo now. I reckon those guns have already

been moved out. If my hunch is right, they're hidden somewhere among those travelers by now."

Angela blinked as what Cody was saying sank in. "The wagons . . ." she said, almost in a whisper.

Nodding, Cody said, "That's what I figure. The gang stole the rifles, brought them to San Antonio, and hid them in the Alamo until they got a chance to move them again. A couple of the prairie schooners probably have false bottoms. That would be enough to handle the crates."

"But you don't have any proof of this?"

"Not a damn bit. But it all ties together, and what better way to smuggle those rifles on west to the Comanches? I don't know if the gang is planning to sell the Winchesters to a band of comancheros or deal directly with the Indians. Either way, when the wagon train gets to a certain spot, I'm willing to bet they'll be met, and the guns will be delivered."

Angela frowned and asked, "What about all the other people on the trip, the settlers who don't have anything to do with the gun smuggling?"

"I reckon they'll all be killed," Cody said quietly. "Those bastards won't want to leave any witnesses behind."

Angela crossed her arms, hugging herself as a slight shudder ran through her. "If you're right, you've got to stop them. But what if you're wrong?"

The Ranger looked at her for a long moment without saying anything; then he sighed. "Looks like it's a roll of the dice, either way. If I keep nosing around here in San Antonio and the guns are really in the wagon train, a lot of innocent folks'll wind up dead. But if I stick with the wagon train and I'm wrong, and the rifles are really still here, that'll be just as bad. So I've got to make a choice and hope it's the right one."

"Have you . . . made that choice?"

Cody nodded. "I'm going to be part of that wagon train when it pulls out in the morning."

"Do you think they'll let you join up at the last minute like that?"

"If they're headed west, they'll be going through
some rugged territory. I think they'll be glad to have
another man who can handle a gun along with them."

Angela started to pace back and forth, her forehead
creasing in thought. "The rest of the men working with
the Grady brothers—this gang, as you call them—
they'll be part of the wagon train," she remarked.

"I can't imagine them not going. They're not about
to trust those rifles to anybody else after bringing them
this far."

"And they're also bound to know about the Gradys
and those other men being dead."

"Reckon they'll have heard the news, all right,"
Cody admitted. "But remember, Uriah Grady didn't
know I was a Ranger till I told him, and I've got a feeling Uriah was the smartest out of those four. The rest
of the gang won't know I'm a lawman."

"But Uriah *could* have told them that someone had
been following him and Calvin. Isn't it possible that
when you show up wanting to join the wagon train at
the last minute, somebody might get suspicious and
connect you with what happened tonight?"

"I suppose it's possible." Cody hesitated, then
asked point-blank, "Just what are you getting at, Angela?"

"You'll have a lot easier time blending in with the
others and getting a chance to look for those guns if
you seem like an actual settler."

"Well, I intend to get a wagon and some supplies to
make it look real. I'm hoping you can point me to
somebody who'll sell me what I need, first thing in the
morning."

"That won't be a problem. I know several places that
can outfit you, and if you're willing to pay extra, the
owners won't mind getting up at the crack of dawn."
She caught at her full lower lip with her even white
teeth. "I was really thinking about something else,

something that would make your presence in the train even less suspicious."

"Sounds good to me," Cody said. "What is it?"

"A wife to go along on the trip with you."

Cody stared at her for a few seconds, his eyes narrowing. "I reckon that might make me look more like just another pilgrim, all right," he finally said. "But one night's pretty short notice to come up with a wife."

"It's not such short notice," Angela said. "I know where you can find a woman to go with you."

Cody figured he knew what she was going to say, so he waited in silence.

"I'll do it."

"You'll pretend to be my wife?"

"Yes. It makes sense, doesn't it?"

"What about your saloon?" Cody asked. "You planning to just close up the Crystal Slipper?"

"Lew can run the place for me," Angela replied. "He's very reliable, and I don't think he'd ever steal from me."

Cody said bluntly, "He's in love with you. Do you think he's going to be agreeable to taking over when he finds out you're going off with another man?"

A slight blush colored Angela's cheeks. "I just won't tell him where I'm going, that's all. I'll tell him that I have to go out of town on business for a few weeks. He'll accept that."

"You're mighty sure of him."

"I'm a good judge of men," she said defiantly. "Well, how about it, Cody? Are you going to take me up on the offer or not? Just how badly do you want to find those rifles?"

She should have known the answer to that question already, he thought. Locating those Winchesters was the most important thing right now. But he still didn't like the idea of exposing her to any more danger than was necessary.

Dammit, though, she was right—the presence of a

wife would make his masquerade as a settler much more believable. He could claim that he and the missus had heard there was a wagon train leaving San Antonio and decided on the spur of the moment to join up. Honest folks would accept them at face value, and likely so would the gun smugglers.

"I'm not overly fond of the idea," the Ranger groused, "but I reckon you've got a point. You sure you want to go through with it?"

"Of course I'm sure," she said, and if she had any hidden doubt, Cody couldn't detect it in her voice. "We'll have to get started very early in the morning," she went on. "Just a few hours from now, in fact. Meet me at five o'clock over on Flores Street, at Hudnall's Wagonyard. That's the best place to buy a wagon. And there's a mercantile right next door, where we can buy supplies. Both Mr. Hudnall and the man who owns the store live in quarters behind their businesses, so we'll be able to rouse them." She smiled. "Like I said, they won't mind getting up early to outfit us, especially when they see the color of your money. You do have enough money, don't you?"

That was another matter that was worrying Cody. He said, "Well, now that you mention it, I don't know if I have enough for such a big undertaking. I suppose I could go roust Major Jones out of bed and maybe come up with the cash—"

Angela stopped him with a casual wave of her hand. "Never mind about that. I've got plenty of money. I'll take care of the bills. You just be ready to travel, Cody."

He could hear the excitement in her voice. Her earlier depression was dropping away before his eyes. Likely she wouldn't sleep much tonight, if at all, he thought.

Turning his hat over in his hands, he said, "You're sure those fellas won't be upset when we come knocking on their doors before sunup?"

Angela gave him a smug smile. "They're customers

of mine," she said. "They'll be glad for the chance to do a favor for me."

"I see."

"No, you probably don't," she said quickly. "I've never brought them back here to the house with me, if that's what you're thinking. But they *are* good friends. And they'll be very discreet, besides."

"Right." He clapped his hat on his head. "Reckon I'd better get moving, then." He hesitated. "One thing . . ."

"Yes?"

"These pilgrims—what if some of them are local folks? Won't they know you—and know you aren't married?"

Angela laughed. "Don't worry. Nearly everyone who heads west from here isn't *from* here—they generally all come from farther back east. And in the unlikely event that there are a few locals among the travelers . . . well, I'm quite sure that even if they know me, they won't *know* me."

He stared at her, puzzled. When she said nothing further, he shrugged and stated, "I'll see you around five on Flores Street."

"I'll be there."

Cody didn't doubt that for a second.

This sure had been a strange night, he thought as he rode slowly back to the Carlton Hotel. He didn't expect to sleep much, either, but he was going to give it a try. Tomorrow—later today, really—would be long and hard if he and Angela succeeded in joining the wagon train.

His left arm hurt a little; diving on the ground and rolling around while the Gradys were shooting at him had made the knife wound start aching again. He massaged the muscles below the wound as he thought about the way Angela had invited herself along with him on this mission. She wasn't a Ranger; she was a saloonkeeper. And for probably the hundredth time since he'd arrived in San Antonio, Cody wondered just what her part in all this really was. That was another reason he'd agreed to her suggestion. Playing along with her was probably the quickest way to find out what she really wanted.

What she wanted wasn't *him,* he was sure of that. Since that first night and the kiss they'd shared, she had kept her distance from him. In fact her excitement tonight as they discussed joining the wagon train was the first real sign of passion he had seen from her in forty-eight hours. They hadn't discussed the more intimate arrangements for the journey they would be making, but he assumed that what she had in mind was to be his wife in name only.

He could live with that—if it helped him round up those Winchesters and the men who had stolen them. But it wasn't going to be easy, sharing a wagon with a woman as beautiful and appealing as Angela Halliday and knowing that she was only interested in him as a Ranger.

The streets were practically deserted at this late hour, and it didn't take long for him to reach the hotel. He put the dun in the corral and hung his saddle on the fence, then went inside, carefully stepping around the sleeping Pedro and Lupe. Cody smiled down at the boys and knelt beside them. He slipped a ten-dollar gold piece into Pedro's hand, then did the same with Lupe. The youngsters stirred a little but didn't wake up. They'd be mighty surprised in the morning when they woke up and found themselves what they'd consider rich. He'd be long gone by then, but he had a feeling the boys would know where the money had come from.

Cody went upstairs, keeping his guard up even though he wasn't expecting any more trouble tonight. He had a hunch the Grady brothers and Fred and Billy were the only members of the gang who even suspected his existence.

His room was empty. He took off his boots, hat,

vest, and gun belt, then stretched out on the bed with the rest of his clothes on. As he was sure Angela's were, his thoughts were full of the plans they'd made, and he also couldn't forget how much was riding on this. He'd told her that making the decision to join the wagon train or not was like a roll of the dice, and that was certainly true. Most of the time he was pretty lucky at games of chance—but not always. Sometimes he lost.

He couldn't afford to lose this time.

Though Cody hadn't expected to get much sleep, he nonetheless dozed off fairly quickly. His mental alarm was reliable, and he awoke with a start just as streaks of gray were beginning to appear in the night sky. Sitting up, he swung his feet out of bed, gave his head a couple of shakes to clear away some of the cobwebs, then stood and stretched.

It was time to play out the hand—maybe the last and most important hand in this game of guns and death—and the dealing started *now*.

By the time the eastern sky started turning pink, Cody was riding slowly along Flores Street. A few people were out and about at this time of day, but not many. He asked a man walking along the sidewalk where Hudnall's Wagonyard was located and was told to keep heading in the direction he was going for another four blocks. A few minutes later Cody saw the building and the large, corraled enclosure to one side of it.

As he drew rein in front of the establishment, Angela emerged from the front door, lantern light behind her. At least Cody assumed the woman was Angela. It took a long second look to be sure.

Gone was the flashy, sensuous, seductive saloonkeeper. In place of a spangled gown was a homespun calico dress and a sunbonnet that at the moment hung from a bow around her neck. Her ash-blond hair was tied neatly in a bun, and her well-scrubbed face wore not a trace of the paint she usually sported. Leaning forward in the saddle and studying her, Cody decided she looked about as fresh and clean and wholesome as any woman he'd ever seen. This was yet another new face for Angela Halliday.

"Good morning," she said brightly as she looked up at him. "I got here a little early, so I went ahead and spoke to Mr. Hudnall about a wagon. He's fixing us up with the best one he has."

"Good mornin' yourself," Cody said, thumbing back his hat. He grinned wryly. "I'm a mite surprised you don't already have our supplies taken care of, too."

Angela returned the grin. "I'm working on it. Why don't you see to the wagon and the team while I go over to the store?"

Cody nodded and swung down from the saddle. "All right. You know what to get?"

"Staples for . . . what? A month?"

"Better make it six weeks, just so it'll look like we intend to make the whole trip," Cody told her after thinking over the question for a few seconds. He reached out and caught her arm as she started past him. "And get something pretty for yourself. A man likes for his wife to have a treat every now and then."

Her eyes flashed in the dawn light, and for a moment Cody thought he'd gone too far. But then she smiled again and murmured, "Of course, *darling*. Considering that *I'm* the one paying for this, I think I do deserve something special."

Cody prodded a tooth with the tip of his tongue, deciding not to press his luck any further. "I'll tend to the wagon," he said.

"You do that." Angela's voice was slightly tart but not unfriendly. Cody stood and watched her for a moment as she walked toward the mercantile, then gave a small shake of his head and went to tend to the rest of the details concerning the wagon.

Hudnall was a florid-faced, thick-bodied man who didn't seem the least bit upset to be called out of his bed this early in the morning to sell a wagon and team. And he wasn't inquisitive, which was another point in his favor as far as Cody was concerned. Hudnall shook hands firmly with the Ranger, then took him into the wagonyard to show him the vehicle. It was a prairie schooner of the usual type, a smaller version of the famous Conestoga. "The wood in that wagon is the finest oak you'll find, sir," Hudnall said proudly. "And the iron reinforcing makes it the strongest vehicle in these parts, too. No, sir, you just can't beat this wagon."

"What about the team?" Cody asked.

"Six of the strongest mules west of the Mississippi! Of course, they are a mite stubborn. Why, you could even say they're—"

"—as stubborn as mules," Cody finished, and Hudnall looked slightly crestfallen that the Ranger had completed the joke for him. Cody hurried on, "We'd better get them hitched up. Angela and I are leaving with that wagon train that's pulling out this morning."

"That's what she told me." Hudnall was obviously curious about who Cody was and why Angela was leaving San Antonio with him, but he didn't ask any questions. He and Cody led the mules from the large barn on the other side of the wagonyard and had them hitched up by the time Angela had returned from the store.

"The order is being gathered up now," she said. "All we have to do is drive by there and pick it up. I've already settled the bill."

"Good," Cody grunted. "I reckon we're ready to go." He tied the dun to the back of the wagon, then walked to the seat and climbed up. Turning, he extended a hand to help Angela. She grasped it, her hand cool and smooth, and he lifted her easily to the box.

Hudnall opened the gate as Cody took the reins and drove out of the yard, swinging the wagon to the left and bringing it to a stop a few yards later in front of the general store. The proprietor was just emerging from the doorway with a box of supplies in his hands, and when he saw the wagon, he continued on across the sidewalk instead of setting his burden down. "Here you go, Angela," he called. "I'll go back for the rest of the goods."

Cody dropped from the seat and took the box from the man. "We're obliged for your help," he said.

"Anything for Angela." The storekeeper grinned. "Within reason, of course."

Cody placed the supplies in the back of the wagon. The merchant brought out two more boxes full of goods, primarily things like flour, sugar, coffee, and beans. Angela had also purchased a hammer, nails, a shovel and hoe, and other tools that might be needed on a journey such as the one they were undertaking. She had done a good job, Cody saw as he loaded the supplies. He knew nothing about her past, but he guessed that she'd made at least one trip by covered wagon sometime in her life.

The vehicle had to be turned around and headed north so that they could drive over to the Alamo and the place where the wagon train had gathered. It'd been a while since Cody had handled a wagon, but the knack of it returned to him fairly quickly once he held the reins. He shouted at the mules and cracked the whip over their heads, and after a few moments they decided to cooperate. Guiding the wagon through the streets reminded Cody of the days he'd driven a wagon on the family ranch, back when his father was still alive.

The sun was about to poke above the horizon as they swung east on Commerce Street, and Cody squinted against the growing glare. It had been about this time of the morning when the six thousand Mexican troops under old Santa Anna himself had stormed the Alamo, he remembered.

Considerably more traffic was on the street now as people headed for their day's work. Cody veered the wagon around other vehicles and men on horseback, as well as the increasing number of pedestrians. Angela sat beside him, close enough so that the wagon's bouncing and swaying made her lean against him occasionally. Cody told himself not to make anything out of that. After all, a wife would normally sit that close to her husband.

He glanced over at her. She had pulled the sunbonnet up now so that it partially hid her face, and even though she looked vastly different from the way she normally did, she also kept her head downcast, obscuring her face even more. As she was fairly well known, she was doing her best to ensure that passersby wouldn't know that the saloonkeeper was leaving town with a stranger. The Ranger was able to catch a glimpse of her face every now and then, however, and he could see that her eyes were still shining with excitement.

"How'd Lew take the news?" Cody asked quietly, not to ruin her good mood but needing to know. Leaving an angry, jealous man behind could sometimes backfire.

"Lew was fine," Angela assured him. "I knew he would be. I just told him I had to go on a business trip, and I'd be back as soon as I could. He didn't ask any questions. He just told me to be careful."

"He seems like a nice fella, all right." Cody hesitated, then went on, "Maybe when you get back, you ought to think about settling down a little—maybe even with somebody like Lew."

She shot a glance at him, her finely chiseled features hardening. "I don't intend to get married, to Lew or anybody else, if that's what you're talking about. My personal life is my own business, Cody."

He shrugged. "Just a suggestion. You do what you want."

"I usually do."

Cody could believe that. Look at the way she had bulled her way into coming along on this assignment with him, he thought. He grunted and flicked the reins at the mules again.

The Alamo came into sight and beyond it the wagon train camp. The place was extremely busy this morning as folks finished their last-minute loading and hitched up their teams to pull the wagons into line. Cody drove

up to the edge of the encampment and hauled back on
the reins, looking for somebody who could tell him
where to find the wagon master. He finally caught the
eye of one of the settlers and hailed the man.

"Mr. Stone's over there," the pilgrim said in reply to
Cody's question and pointing toward the front of the
caravan, which was rapidly acquiring a distinct shape
as opposed to being simply a mass of wagons.

"Thanks, pard," Cody said, then headed his own vehicle toward the spot. As they approached, the Ranger
saw a man on a fine Appaloosa stallion riding from
wagon to wagon, checking to make sure its occupants
were ready to go. The rider wore buckskins, high-
topped boots, and a wide-brimmed black hat that had
seen better days. His saddle and the holster in which a
Remington .44 rode were well cared for, though, Cody
could see at a glance. Stone was middle-aged but still
vigorous and powerful-looking. His skin had the leathery color and texture common to a man who's spent
most of his life outdoors, and his short beard was
grizzled with silver.

His dark eyes snapped angrily when he noticed
Cody and Angela approaching, and he turned toward
them, shouting, "What the hell're you doin' out of
line? We're movin' out in five minutes!"

"Sorry, mister," Cody said, reining in again. "I
don't reckon we've got a place in line yet."

"You don't have a place . . . ? Say, do I know you?"

Cody shook his head. "Nope. The missus and I just
got here. We're hoping to join your wagon train."

"Well, why in blazes didn't you say so?" the wagon
master demanded irascibly. "What's your name?"

"Sam Cole," Cody said. He'd decided that he
wanted to leave his identity as Sam Carson behind
when they left. He inclined his head toward the woman
beside him. "This's my wife, Angela."

Stone lifted a knobby finger to the drooping brim of
his hat. "Ma'am," he acknowledged tersely. Turning
his attention back to Cody, he asked, "Do you even
know where we're bound?"

"Doesn't matter. We're looking to make a new start."

"Law ain't after you, is it, Cole?" Stone asked with a suspicious frown. He moved his hand closer to the butt of the .44 on his hip.

"Not hardly," Cody replied with a laugh. "We just want to leave behind some bad memories. Our farm failed."

Stone leaned over and stared pointedly at the Colt on Cody's hip. "Can you use that?" He gestured toward the gun.

"Well enough. I've got a Winchester rifle, too."

"Well, we're headin' into country where there may be some trouble from Injuns and renegades, white and Mex alike. A man's got to be willin' to fight."

"I'm willing to do whatever it takes," Cody said softly.

The wagon master leaned on the saddle horn and switched his attention to Angela. "That go for you, too, ma'am?"

"Of course it does, Mr. Stone," she replied. "I've always supported my husband in everything he does."

Stone nodded abruptly. "All right, then. I reckon we'll be glad to have you with us, as long as you abide by the rules and don't cause no trouble. Ain't no time to fool with the papers you got to sign when you join up, but we can take care of that at the noon stop. Since you're the last ones to get here, you'll have to eat dust. Bein' last in line, you'll have to be careful not to get too far behind. Nothin' a bunch of bloodthirsty Injuns like better'n a straggler." He kneed his horse closer to the wagon and held out a hand. "I'm Caleb Stone, the wagon master. Reckon you've figured that last part out. Glad to have you with us, folks."

Cody shook Stone's hand. The grip was firm and strong, which came as no surprise. Caleb Stone looked and sounded like a seasoned veteran of the frontier.

The wagon master doffed his hat to Angela for a second, then wheeled his horse and went on about his last-minute chores. Cody got the wagon turned around

again—a trickier proposition here with all the other vehicles—and headed for the rear of the train. He'd halfway expected to be given the last position, and if there
was one thing certain about this journey it was that he
and Angela would have to get used to dust.

Something was nagging at Cody's brain as he drove
the wagon toward its assigned position at the tail end of
the group. He realized he was frowning when Angela
whispered, "What's wrong?"

Cody hesitated before framing his answer, then said
slowly, "Something about Stone seems familiar to
me."

"You might have seen him around town. Or you
could have run into him somewhere else, sometime in
the past. He struck me as a man who's been around a
great deal."

"Reckon that's true enough. But it's not the way he
looks. It's his name. Caleb Stone . . ." Cody mused.
"I'm sure I've heard of him before."

"Maybe it'll come to you."

Cody shrugged. If it was important, he would think
of it sooner or later.

They drew quite a few curious looks from the other
travelers as they made their way to the rear of the
wagon train. Several children smiled and waved from
wagon boxes, and Cody and Angela made a point of
returning greetings. This was a good-sized caravan for
the day and age, with several dozen wagons, and Cody
estimated that well over a hundred people would be
making the journey.

Somewhere among them were the thieves who had
stolen the army rifles. Cody told himself that had to be
true, otherwise he and Angela were wasting their
time—and practically putting those Winchesters in the
hands of the Comanches.

If his hunch about the weapons was right, though,
rooting them out would still be a difficult chore. The
more friends he and Angela could make on the trip, the
more likely they'd be to uncover the other members of
the gang. He was counting on that.

The memory suddenly flashed into Cody's brain as he maneuvered the wagon into line. "Damn!" The quiet exclamation burst out of him as he recalled where he had heard Caleb Stone's name before.

"What is it?" Angela asked anxiously.

Cody leaned over slightly, looking far toward the front of the line where the lead wagons were already pulling out into the street. He spotted Stone's distinctive mount. The wagon master was sitting to one side and watching the wagons depart from their camp.

"Now I know why Stone's name sounded familiar. I've heard some of the older Rangers talking about him."

"Was he a lawman, too?" Angela asked.

"Not hardly. Although there's plenty in Texas who'd say he wasn't really an outlaw, either. He used to be a smuggler, back during the War Between the States. The Union Navy had the Gulf Coast blockaded, so men like Stone brought guns and ammunition and food across the Rio Grande from Mexico into Texas. The Yankees tried to stop them, of course, but they never managed to corral Stone. He made plenty of money for himself, but he helped keep some people from starving when times were bad. Reckon that's why, once Davis's carpetbaggers and reconstructionists got booted out, the law never really went after Stone."

Angela clutched Cody's arm as the import of his story sank in on her. "If Stone used to be a smuggler . . ."

"That's right," Cody said. "If anybody knows about transporting stolen goods across the frontier, Caleb Stone's the man."

CHAPTER
7

By the middle of the day Cody had remembered just how sore a man's rear end could get from bouncing up and down on a hard wooden wagon seat for hours. He could ride from dawn to dusk in a saddle without half as much discomfort. From the look on Angela Halliday's face, she was experiencing the same pain.

"Is Stone ever going to call a halt?" she asked, a note of despair in her voice.

Cody glanced up at the sun. "Not quite noon yet," he replied. "Why don't you climb on back and make a place for yourself among those supplies—or even stretch out on the bunk? You might be more comfortable."

She thought about it for a moment, then shook her head. "I'll stay up here with you," she said, sighing. "After all, I'm supposed to be your devoted wife."

Cody chuckled but didn't say anything.

Finally, Caleb Stone rode back alongside the line of wagons, his right hand raised to signal a halt. "Noon stop, folks!" he called. "We'll eat and rest the teams for an hour."

Gratefully, Cody hauled the mules in and then dropped off the wagon box, staggering a little from stiff muscles as he landed. In a day or two he'd start getting used to traveling like this, he knew, but until then the journey wouldn't be too pleasant.

He reached up and helped Angela down from the wagon. She sagged against him for a moment as he set her on the ground, and he was well aware of the warmth of her flesh where his hands gripped her around her trim waist. They stood there like that as several seconds went by, and then Angela pulled away.

"I'd better get busy fixing us something to eat," she said without looking at him.

Cody picked up the wooden bucket that was hanging from a hook on the side of the wagon. "I'll get some water for the mules and the dun."

He figured they had only covered about seven or eight miles, a slow pace that probably wouldn't get much faster due to the length of the train. San Antonio still seemed close behind them. In fact, there were as yet quite a few adobe houses along the road that eventually became Commerce Street not many miles back eastward. Stone had picked a good place to stop for a while, Cody saw as he studied the terrain. A creek was nearby, and the road was lined with tall cottonwoods to provide shade. The travelers could pass a fairly pleasant hour here.

Cody joined the other men and women dipping water from the creek to take back to their teams. Children ran around playing, and Cody had to grin at their antics. Kids were the same everywhere, he thought, full of piss and vinegar and ready to have a good time no matter what the circumstances.

The Ranger sleeved sweat off his forehead as he waited his turn for water. The weather had started to heat up as soon as the sun was over the horizon, and the air seemed to get hotter and drier as the day went on. The brief rain of the night before had done little to help, being sucked up rapidly by the thirsty ground. Cody frowned, wondering if Stone had considered postponing the journey until this dry spell broke. It mightn't be too wise to start across the southern Texas plains in weather like this.

Unless Stone had some other reason for leaving San Antonio when he had—such as delivering two hundred stolen rifles to some impatient buyers.

Cody scowled. He could be jumping to conclusions. There were plenty of streams between here and the Rio

Grande. A few of them might be running low from the lack of rain, but he doubted that any of them would be dried up. If the stories Cody had heard about Caleb Stone were true, the man knew this part of the country like the back of his hand. He'd know the best route, the trails where water would be available.

Concentrating his attention on Stone because of the wagon master's background might backfire on him, Cody told himself. Better to keep his eyes wide open and trust nobody.

Back at the wagon, Angela had built a small fire and was laying strips of bacon in one of their pans. She had biscuit dough mixed in another pan, using some of the water from one of the canteens in the wagon to prepare it, and a pot of beans was simmering on the flames. She was kneeling beside the fire with the bacon when a voice said, "You won't be able to fix such nice meals for your husband once we really get started on the trail, honey."

Angela looked up to see a woman in a green dress and bonnet standing there, a smile on her face. The stranger was perhaps a dozen years older than Angela, and her face was rather lined and weathered, telltale signs of a hard life, but she retained an attractiveness that said she had been quite a beauty in her day. Brown hair touched with gray curled from under the bonnet.

"Excuse me?" Angela said.

"I was just saying you won't be able to fix anything this fancy once the wagon train gets started good," the woman replied. "Not for lunch, anyway. Mr. Stone won't let us stop long enough to build fires and such. You'll eat biscuits and jerky for your noon meal, right there on the wagon seat."

Angela moved the pot of beans over slightly and got the bacon cooking, too. She stood up and brushed her hands off. "You're right," she agreed. "I've traveled with a wagon train before; I know things will get harder as we go along."

The other woman held her hand out. "I'm Margaret Duncan. My friends call me Meg."

Angela hesitated slightly, then took her hand. "My name's Angela Cole," she said.

"I'm mighty pleased to meet you, Mrs. Cole. It is Mrs., isn't it?"

Smiling a little at the way Meg Duncan was blatantly pumping her for information, Angela said, "Yes, it certainly is. I'm traveling with my husband, Sam."

"Just the two of you? No young'uns?"

Angela shook her head. "No. We . . . don't have any children."

"Got four myself. Four that lived, that is. Four more didn't. But life was mighty difficult back then, you've got to understand. Homer and I always felt blessed that we got the ones we did. They're all grown up now, married and everything."

"Is your family with you?" Angela asked, keeping an eye on the cooking food.

"No, I'm by myself. Homer passed away about two years ago, rest his soul. And you couldn't get those young'uns of mine to leave their nice homes. I reckon they're just not as fiddle-footed as their mama is."

It came as no surprise to Angela that Meg was traveling alone. She had immediately pegged the older woman as lonely—undoubtedly the reason she had come over from her own wagon and started a conversation with a stranger. But Angela was curious enough to ask, "Doesn't it bother you, setting out on a trip by yourself like that?"

Meg smiled again. "Honey, I've herded cattle alongside my husband from can to cain't. I've fought fevers and cholera when there wasn't a real doctor within fifty miles. I've shot a Comanche warrior about two seconds before he was going to lift the hair from one of my babies." She shook her head. "A little trip to California doesn't amount to much when you've lived a life like that."

Angela nodded slowly. "I can see why you feel that

way. California . . . she mused. "Is that where we're going?"

"Land sakes, girl, you mean you don't even know where you're bound for?"

"We left in a hurry." She went on quickly, "There was no trouble, you understand. It's just that our farm failed, and my husband wants to make a new start somewhere else with what money we have left."

"Reckon I can understand that." Meg patted Angela on the arm. "You'll do fine, just fine. I've been around this frontier long enough to know good folks when I see 'em. I'm sure your mister's the same way."

"I think so. . . ." Angela's voice trailed off.

"This must be him coming now."

Angela turned to see Cody striding toward the wagon, the bucket filled with creek water dangling from his left hand. His right, as usual, wasn't very far from the butt of his gun.

Seeing Angela talking to the stranger as he approached, Cody wondered who the older woman was. She had to be one of the other travelers, he supposed. That was good. He planned for them to meet everyone else in the train before this journey was over.

He set the bucket on the ground as he came up to the two women. Tugging his hat off, he nodded and said to the stranger, "Howdy, ma'am."

Angela took his arm, squeezing it a little harder than she needed to, Cody thought. Quickly, she performed the introductions.

"Pleased to meet you, Mr. Cole," Meg Duncan said to him. "I've just been talking to your wife here. She's a mighty sweet girl."

Cody glanced down at Angela and said with a smile, "I've always thought so."

Her fingers tightened on his arm again, almost painfully this time. She asked, "Would you like to join us for lunch, Meg? I'm sure there'll be plenty."

"Oh, no, thank you anyway. I've got a mess of hardtack and jerky. No, I'll leave you folks alone. As alone as you can get, leastways, in the middle of this many wagons and people and mules." Meg smiled slyly. "You got the look of newlyweds to me."

"We've been married about ten months," Cody said, "so I reckon we are still newlyweds." He turned to Angela. "Aren't we?"

She slipped an arm around his waist. "Of course."

Meg started back to her own wagon, turning to give them a wave as she left. Cody and Angela stood there until the Ranger realized their pose was starting to look a little awkward. He stepped away from Angela, nodded toward the food, and said, "We'd better eat. Stone'll have us on the road again before you know it."

"Yes," Angela said, her face expressionless now. "I suppose he will."

And a good thing, too, Cody thought. This idea of pretending to be husband and wife had sounded fine starting out. He just hoped it didn't turn out to be more trouble than he'd bargained for.

Cody watered the mules, and by the time he'd finished, Angela had the biscuits and bacon and beans ready. The Ranger ate hungrily. Handling a team of mules and a wagon was hard work, and it took a lot out of a man. He washed the food down with water, wishing that Angela had thought to brew up a pot of Arbuckle's. Well, they could have coffee with supper, he supposed.

When the meal was over, Cody sat down under one of the cottonwoods and stretched out his legs, grateful for the opportunity to rest for a few minutes. He'd barely gotten settled down when Angela said to him, "Why don't you take these pans down to the creek and wash them?"

Cody glared at her, then sighed and pushed himself back to his feet. The woman was taking this damn marriage business too far, he muttered to himself as he took the pans and headed for the stream.

A short while later, Caleb Stone rode among the settlers and told them to start getting ready to move again. Cody and Angela were already prepared. They climbed onto the wagon box, and when the long line of canvas-covered vehicles lurched into motion again, Cody cracked the whip and urged the team of mules into a plodding walk. More dust, more bouncing, more aches and pains, he groaned inwardly . . . but it would all be worthwhile if he could find those guns and keep them from getting to the Indians.

Around the middle of the afternoon, Angela's lack of sleep the night before and the unaccustomed exertion got to be too much for her, and she decided to retreat into the shade of the wagon bed for a nap. Cody thought it was a good idea and told her as much. "You're not used to this heat," he explained. "You'd be better off out of the sun for a while."

"Well, I feel I'm deserting you," Angela protested.

Cody shook his head. "Not at all. I can handle this wagon and these mules just fine, Angela. Now, go get some rest."

She nodded wearily, climbed over the back of the seat, and disappeared behind him.

Cody took his hat off and sleeved sweat from his forehead, then took his bandanna and ran it around the inside of the Stetson's headband. Despite what he had told Angela, the heat and the hard work of driving the wagon were taking their toll. He looked ahead at the long line of wagons stretched out in front of him. The day was just as hot and hard for those folks as it was for him—harder, no doubt, because he was used to leading an active life in the outdoors. Not for the first time the Ranger was struck by the sheer grit of settlers like these who braved outlaws and Indians and the elements and all kinds of other hardships just so they could try to carve a place for themselves out of the frontier. It took a lot more courage to face something like that, he told himself, than it did to be a Ranger.

Angela reappeared about an hour later, looking slightly less tired. She gave Cody a smile and asked, "Would you like me to take over the reins for a while?"

He looked over at her. "You can handle a team of mules?"

"Well, it's been a long time since I've done anything like that . . . but I can try."

Cody shrugged and passed the reins over to her. "You've got to make sure they know you're still there. Otherwise they'll take it in their heads to stop."

She nodded and tightened her grip on the lines.

Cody straightened his spine, easing some of the stiffness in his back. Watching Angela driving the wagon, his admiration for her grew as he saw the way she kept the mules moving by flicking the reins against their backs fairly often. She even pulled the whip from its socket and cracked it a couple of times as she shouted at the animals. It might've been a while since she'd handled a team like this, Cody thought, but the skill had come back to her in a hurry.

Cody had initially figured the wagon train might reach the Medina River by nightfall, but the pace was too slow for that. He estimated they were still several miles east of that stream when Stone called a halt. Another small creek was flowing nearby, though, and the wagons turned off the trail to make camp beside it. This close to San Antonio, it was highly unlikely they would encounter any hostile Indians, so Stone didn't bother instructing the settlers to pull their wagons into a circle for protection. Later, as they got farther west, such precautions would become a matter of course.

While Cody unhitched the mules and gave them grain and water, Angela began preparing their supper. After the dun had also been fed and watered, Cody hobbled the horse and the mules for the night. The smell of coffee brewing floated to Cody's nose, and he drew a deep breath, tired but satisfied with the progress they'd made so far. They seemed to have been accepted as members of the wagon train; tonight he'd start the work of poking around the camp and seeing what he could find out.

He strode over to their cooking fire. The fare wasn't going to vary much while they were on the trail, Cody knew. Most meals would consist of beans, bacon, and

biscuits. He might be able to shoot some game along
the way, so that they could have rabbit or venison instead of bacon, but that would likely be the only varia-
tion.

"How's supper coming?" he asked Angela.

"It'll be a while before it's ready."

Nodding, he said, "Think I'll wander around the
camp a little, maybe get to know some of the folks."

She glanced up at him, and he could tell from the
look in her eyes that she knew what he was up to. "Be
careful," she said quietly.

He gave her a reassuring smile, then strolled along
the banks of the creek past the other wagons. Nearly
every family had a cooking fire going, so there was
plenty of light even though the shadows of night had
begun to fall over the plains. Cody exchanged greetings
with several people who nodded at him in a friendly
manner. He was invited to share supper with a couple
of families but politely declined, saying that his wife
was preparing their meal back at their wagon.

Angela's suggestion that he bring a wife along on this
trip made even more sense to him now. Almost every
man he saw seemed to be married, and most of them
had children, too. It was doubtful that the gun smugglers would have brought their families along, if they
even had families, so he was on the lookout for men
traveling alone. They'd be the most likely suspects.

Glancing toward the center of the camp, Cody
spotted the tent that had been pitched by Caleb Stone
and wandered in that direction. Since the wagon master didn't have a vehicle of his own, he had brought
along a tent that during the day was stowed in one of
the wagons that had enough available room. Stone
didn't have his own cooking fire going, either; he'd
take his meals with various families—a fairly common
setup for wagon masters.

Stone hadn't brought the papers for Cody to sign
during the noon halt as he had said he would, and the
Ranger figured the matter had slipped Stone's mind.
He wanted to get that taken care of so that he and An-

gela would be official members of the company. But there was no sign of Stone around his tent, and Cody didn't see him at any of the nearby wagons.

This might be a good opportunity to take a look in Stone's tent, Cody suddenly realized. If anybody noticed him poking around, he could claim that he was looking for the wagon master in order to take care of the paperwork. Striding boldly up to the tent, Cody brushed aside the canvas flap covering the entrance and, as he stepped inside, called, "Mr. Stone?"

As he had assumed, no one was in the tent. A bedroll was slung on the ground in one corner, and a pair of saddlebags had been tossed down beside it. Cody hesitated, then stepped over to the saddlebags. He was just reaching down to pick them up when the sound of voices outside made him pause. Stone could walk in here without any warning and catch him, and so could anybody else. It was too early in the journey to be taking such risks. As soon as the passing voices had died away, Cody thrust back the canvas and stepped outside.

A heavy hand came down on his shoulder. The Ranger tensed, ready to reach for the gun on his hip. As he jerked his head around to see who had grabbed him, a deep voice said, "Hold on there, son. No need to get excited. I just want to know what you were doing in our wagon master's tent."

The other man was as tall as Cody, and their eyes met squarely in the light from the cooking fires. The stranger's shoulders were broad, and the ruggedness of his features showed that he had been in more than one fight in his life. He wasn't wearing a hat, and the evening breeze along the creek plucked at the thatch of black hair on his head. His dark suit had been lightened considerably by trail dust, and his white shirt was buttoned to the throat, even though he wasn't wearing a tie of any sort. The long, supple fingers of the hand that gripped Cody's shoulder possessed a surprising strength.

Cody shrugged, seemingly nonchalant, but the gesture contained enough power to shake the hand off his shoulder. "I was looking for Mr. Stone," he said. "Reckon that'd be obvious."

"It would be, if Mr. Stone was in there," the man retorted. "But he's not. I saw him heading over to the Chadwick wagon for supper."

"I didn't know that. I wasn't trying to steal anything, if that's what you're worried about."

The man grinned suddenly. "Who said I was worried? It's just that on a trip like this, folks have to watch out for each other. If you're an honest man, you've got no quarrel with me." He extended the hand he had used to grasp Cody's shoulder. "I'm Josiah Croft."

Cody took the hand. "Sam Cole. Glad to meet you, Croft . . . I reckon."

Croft chuckled. "Going to California, are you?"

"Maybe," Cody replied with a shrug. "Unless I find a spot on the way that suits me and the missus better."

"Oh, you're traveling with your family, then?"

"It's just me and my wife." Cody fell in alongside Croft as the older man started to stroll toward the edge of the camp. "What about you?"

Croft shook his head. "I'm not married. A man in my line of work, traveling around as much as I do . . ."

When it became evident that Croft didn't intend to finish the sentence, Cody indulged his curiosity and asked, "What line of work would that be?"

Before Croft could answer, a voice hailed Cody from behind. "There you are, Cole," Caleb Stone said as he came up to the two men. "Miz Chadwick said it'd be a while 'fore supper was ready, so I figured I'd find you and get you to sign this here paper." The wagon master held out the contract.

Cody took the document, saying, "I was just looking for you for the same reason, Mr. Stone." He scanned the writing. It was a standard wagon-train contract saying that the undersigned and his family, if any, agreed to abide by the rules of the train, follow the orders of the wagon master, contribute to the common defense, and such. Cody reached into his pocket, took out a stub of pencil, and scrawled *Sam Cole* across the bottom of the paper before handing it back. He then handed Stone the money for the fee.

"Sorry I forgot to get you to do this at noon," Stone said, folding the contract and slipping it and the bills into the pocket of his buckskin shirt. "It plumb slipped my mind." He glanced at Croft. "I see you've met Josiah."

"That's right," Croft said heartily. "I made Mr. Cole's acquaintance when he was looking for you, Caleb." Cody noticed that he didn't say anything about finding the Ranger coming out of Stone's tent. Croft turned back to him and went on, "I'd better get back to my wagon. It was nice meeting you, Mr. Cole."

"Same here," Cody responded.

Stone said his good-byes, too, leaving Cody to make his way back to his own wagon. The Ranger kept an eye on Croft as the man strode briskly toward two wagons that were parked at the edge of the camp. Several men were waiting there, gathered around the cooking fire, but Cody didn't see any women or children.

He frowned in thought as he started to amble toward his and Angela's spot. A group of men traveling alone in a pair of wagons—that fit the description Cody had worked up in his mind of the gun smugglers. They wouldn't have any women or children around to complicate matters, and they'd need at least two wagons with false bottoms to accommodate those crates of rifles.

And Josiah Croft hadn't answered when Cody asked him what sort of work he did.

Of course, all of that could be strictly coincidence, and Cody knew it. But before this journey was too much farther along, he decided, he wanted a look inside those two wagons.

Angela had supper ready by the time he got back. As she handed him a plate full of food, she asked quietly, "Did you find out anything?"

Cody shook his head. "Not really. Maybe got a hunch or two, but nothing solid yet." Quickly, he told her about Croft and the other men who were traveling with him. "I didn't get a very good look at them, but they struck me as pretty hard-bitten." He paused and shook his head. "But maybe that's just what I wanted to see."

"I'll find out if Meg Duncan can tell me anything about this man Croft. She was over here again earlier, and she seems to know a lot of the people in the company. She was camped there in San Antonio the whole time the train was being formed."

"Good idea," Cody said, nodding. "I reckon I probably haven't seen everybody in camp yet, but Croft and his pards are the most likely ones I've run across so far. He and Stone seemed to be friends, too, and that could mean something." He looked down at his plate and realized he had been eating without really being aware of it. "This is mighty good, Angela. I hope you don't think I'm not appreciative."

She smiled and poured a cup of coffee for him. "Don't worry about that. I know you've got a lot on your mind, Sam."

As far as he could recall, this was the first time she had used his given name. He'd always preferred being addressed simply as Cody, but on an assignment like this one that involved a false identity, it was better that she get in the habit of calling him Sam. They could wind up in a situation where a slip such as referring to him as Cody could be dangerous, maybe even fatal.

"Where'd you learn to cook on the trail like this?" he asked. "Not in the Crystal Slipper, that's for sure."

"I had a life before that saloon, Sam." She cocked an eyebrow and smiled sweetly at him. "I know all sorts of things."

He sipped his coffee and said under his breath, "I'll just bet you do."

When they had finished with the meal, Cody took the pans down to the creek and rinsed them without being asked. He took his time about it, using the chore as an excuse to study the camp a bit more as he walked to and from the stream. Quite a few of the fires had burned down to embers, and people were turning in for the night. It had been a long day, and everyone was tired. Some had crawled into their wagons to sleep while others had spread their bedrolls underneath the vehicles. Cody assumed that that was where he would spend the night. He and Angela had to share a wagon, but given the way she had behaved back in San Antonio, he didn't expect her to carry the husband-and-wife act all the way to the makeshift bunk in the back of the wagon. Under the wagon was fine for him, though; he had slept in a lot of worse places. And they would come up with some reason or other to explain why they slept apart to their fellow travelers.

Angela was already inside when he got back. He stepped to the rear of the wagon and held out the clean pans, saying, "Here you go. Since you're already in there, you can put these away."

The light from the dying fire didn't reach the front of the wagon. Angela emerged from the shadows there and said, "All right. You're coming in, aren't you, Sam?"

Cody tried not to stare. The illumination wasn't the best in the world, but it was good enough for him to see that she had removed the dress she was wearing earlier. Now she was clad in a simple cotton nightgown, with her blond hair loose and falling to her shoulders. Cody took a deep breath as he drank in the sight of her.

She leaned over to take the pans from him and hissed, "Don't just stand there. You've got to come in. We can't do anything to make someone suspect even for a moment that we're not what we're supposed to be."

"Happily married," Cody murmured.

"Exactly."

He nodded, then grasped the rear gate of the wagon and swung himself up into the canvas-shrouded interior. There wasn't room for him to stand up, even after he took off his hat, so he waited there on one knee. Angela did something with the pans and then slipped over to him, resting her hands on his chest as she knelt in front of him.

"You don't have to do this," Cody said quietly. "We can both sleep in that bunk without anything else happening."

"I know," she whispered. "But somehow it doesn't seem right. . . ." She lifted her head, found his lips with hers.

The kiss started out warm and tender and stayed that way for a long time, Cody tasting the sweet softness of her lips as he slid his arms around her and drew her closer. Her hands came up and encircled his neck, and for the briefest instant he thought what a good time this would be for her to slip a knife into his back. But if that was what she had in mind, she'd had far better chances to kill him before now. For the moment he was just going to have to trust her.

Especially because the kiss was becoming more intense, her lips opening under his as his tongue caressed them. Her breasts were flattened against his chest, and he could feel the nipples prodding him through her thin cotton nightdress and his work shirt. He slid one hand down her body to the swell of her hips, lingering in the small of her back to massage the muscles there. She pressed harder against him, the softness of her belly molded now to his growing desire.

She let herself fall backward onto the bunk, taking Cody with her. He didn't put up a fight. Her fingers were suddenly working at his pants buttons, tugging and unfastening as she labored to remove all the obstacles between them. When finally nothing was standing in the way, he joined with her. Angela gasped against his mouth.

The lovemaking didn't last long, but it was good. Cody sensed a need in her, a yearning that he wanted to answer. Angela stifled her cries of passion against his chest. There was nothing practiced or artificial about her responses, as he might have expected from the brassy hoyden he'd first thought her to be. From the way she showered kisses on him and whispered urgently in his ear, he figured whatever she was feeling was genuine. And though he had no experience in the area of marriage, he had a feeling she was acting like a woman who was making passionate love with her husband.

When it was over they were both breathless. Angela snuggled against his side, resting her head on his shoulder. It felt damn good to slip his arm around her and hold her tightly, Cody thought. His lips curved in a slow smile in the darkness. He could probably get used to this . . . if he could only figure out just which of the two women he had seen so far—the wanton saloonkeeper or the passionate frontier wife—Angela Halliday really was.

CHAPTER
8
|||||||||||||||||||||||||||||| |||||||||||||||||||||||||||||||

When Angela Halliday awoke the next morning, she stretched for a moment and then rolled over, throwing out an arm to wrap it around the man beside her. But there was no one there, and Angela sat up sharply, her eyes jerking open. "Jim?" she called in a soft, frightened voice.

There was no answer, of course. There never would be again.

Angela took a deep breath and closed her eyes tightly to keep the tears from welling out. Jim wasn't here—and neither was Sam Cody.

Obviously, the Ranger had slipped out of the wagon earlier, while she was still asleep. Hurrying to the rear of the wagon, Angela pushed aside the flap of canvas that hung there for privacy and looked out. A few people were already up and about, although the gray light of approaching dawn was just beginning to filter into the camp, but Cody was nowhere in sight, and Angela had no idea where he had gone. She sat down on one of their boxes of supplies. Her pulse was starting to race, and she willed it to slow down. She was sure Cody was fine; he'd probably just gone off into the bushes to tend to the needs of nature. There was no reason at all for her to think he was never coming back.

But what would happen if indeed he *had* disappeared? That would probably mean he'd run afoul of the gang that had stolen the rifles and been killed by them. She'd be left alone. Angela had no intention of continuing on with the wagon train under those circumstances. She'd have to get back to San Antonio on her own somehow, and as quickly as possible, so that she could alert Major Jones about what had happened.

Aloud she said, "You're just scaring yourself for no good reason, Angela. Sam is perfectly all right, and he'll be back soon."

She wished she could believe that.

Deciding she wasn't doing anyone any good by sitting there and working herself into a state of agitation, Angela quickly moved to the small trunk she'd brought along and selected a fresh dress. She slipped out of the nightgown and pulled the dress on, then reached for her shoes and bonnet. At least while Cody was gone, she could be accomplishing something. Their canteens needed to be filled, she remembered. A quick trip down to the creek would take care of that.

Four canteens hung at the back of the wagon. Angela shook each one of them in turn. One was still full, but two were mostly empty and a third was only half full. She would top off all of them, she decided. Picking up the canteens by the leather thongs attached to them, she climbed out.

Angela kept an eye out for Cody as she walked down to the creek. Her tension grew when she didn't spot him anywhere around the camp. Needing to see a friendly face, she looked around for Meg Duncan as well, but there was no sign of the middle-aged widow, either. Angela took a deep breath and sternly commanded herself to stop worrying. When she reached the creek, she knelt on the bank and leaned over to dip the canteens into the water.

A footfall close behind her made her jump slightly. Then a man's voice said quickly, "I'm sorry! I didn't mean to startle you. I was just going to say good morning."

Angela was balanced precariously on the edge of the stream, and as she started to turn to see who had spoken, she felt her balance deserting her. She flung an arm out, trying to catch herself, but she would have fallen into the creek anyway if the stranger hadn't leapt forward and caught her other arm in a strong grip.

"Be careful!" he said. "I'd never forgive myself if I was the cause of a pretty lady like you falling into a creek!"

With the man's hand steadying her, Angela straightened up, maintaining her hold on the canteens with one hand while the other pushed back a strand of blond hair that had fallen in her face. "I—I'm sorry," she said. "I didn't mean to react like that. I'm sure you meant no offense."

"None at all," the man assured her. "Let me introduce myself. My name is Willard Morgan."

Angela hesitated, then said, "I'm Angela Cole." As she supplied her name, she studied Willard Morgan. He was an inch or so shorter than Cody, which meant he was still a little above medium height, and he was undeniably handsome, with regular features, a shock of brown hair, and long sideburns. The light was still too faint for her to be sure what color his eyes were, but she thought they were green. He kept smiling, which made him look even more charming.

Gesturing at the canteens, he suggested, "Why don't you let me carry those back to your wagon for you?"

"Thank you, but I . . . I still have to finish filling them."

"Well, let me help you do that, then." Without waiting for her to answer, Morgan took the canteens and knelt to finish the chore for her. When the canteens were full and he had fastened their caps tightly, he added, "Now, since I've already got them, there's no point in me not carrying them for you, is there?"

Angela found herself smiling back at him. "I suppose not."

She started toward the wagons. Willard Morgan fell in step beside her. He said, "I hope you won't think I'm being too forward, Miss Cole, but when I saw you going down to the creek, I just had to come over and bid you good morning. Beautiful women seem to have that effect on me."

"It's Mrs. Cole," Angela said. "And you are being a bit forward, Mr. Morgan."

"Only a bit?" He chuckled. "Well, I shall have to try harder."

She should have been angry with him, Angela knew, but his friendly grin made that difficult. He was obviously attracted to her, despite the fact that she was supposed to be married. From his voice she had him pegged as an Easterner—and someone more likely to be found behind a desk than out on the trail. His brown suit looked new and remarkably well kept after a day on the trail, though perhaps he had put it on fresh this morning, just as she had the dress. His cream-colored Stetson looked new, too. As far as she could tell, he wasn't carrying a gun.

"Are you traveling with your family, Mr. Morgan?" she asked.

"I'm afraid I'm not blessed with a family. I'm traveling alone. I suppose that's why I've been looking for some new friends. This godforsaken country can be quite lonely."

"You don't like Texas?"

He shrugged. "I suppose it's all right—if you're a rattlesnake or a scorpion. No, the lush green fields of California, that's my destination. I've been working in Houston for the past couple of years, you see. I went there from Philadelphia. I'm a businessman, and I'd been told that a man could make his fortune in Texas these days. An erroneous declaration, I assure you. So I closed my store in Houston, rode a stagecoach to San Antonio—a perfectly hideous experience—and joined this wagon train for California. I hope to establish some sort of business there; if I'm not successful at that, I'll try my hand at something else."

Listening to him talk, Angela thought he certainly enjoyed the sound of his own voice.

Morgan had paused, but it was only for a moment.

Then he asked, "What sort of work does your husband do?"

"We had a farm for a while, but Sam has done lots of other things. I suppose you could say he's a jack-of-all-trades."

"A good thing to be. Do you have children?"

Angela shook her head. "No, there's just the two of us. We've been married less than a year." Morgan was inquisitive, she thought, asking more questions than folks around this part of the country usually did. No doubt they did things differently back East.

"I'm sure you'll raise a fine family someday. I have to meet this husband of yours. Even without knowing him, I can tell he's a lucky devil." Morgan's smile widened. "Any man who's married to you would have to be lucky, you see."

"I understood what you meant," Angela said dryly. "Well, there's my wagon—" She broke off, her heart beginning to pound again. Cody was standing beside the vehicle, a look of concern on his face. Angela went on, "And there's my husband."

She and Morgan walked up to Cody. The Ranger studied Morgan for a moment, then turned to Angela. "I didn't know where you were," he said. Nodding toward the canteens in Morgan's hands, he continued, "Reckon I know now."

"I didn't want to pass up the opportunity to fill the canteens," she said. "And I didn't know where *you* were, either. When I woke up you were gone."

"Had to go tend to some things," Cody replied somewhat gruffly. He reached for the canteens. "I'll take those, fella."

"Of course. Here you are, my good man." Morgan handed over the canteens.

Cody looked as though he wanted to make some caustic reply to that comment, but he kept his mouth shut. Instead, after a few seconds, he asked, "Any trouble?"

Angela shook her head. "No. I met Mr. Morgan down by the creek, and he helped me." It would be better, she thought, not to say anything about the way he had taken her arm to keep her from falling in or the things he had said to her on their way back to the wagon.

"Much obliged," Cody said to Morgan with a nod.

"It was my pleasure, I assure you." The Easterner turned to Angela and swept his hat off in a gallant gesture. "Good day, Mrs. Cole. I hope the hours pass pleasantly for you."

"Why, thank you, Mr. Morgan." She hesitated, then asked, "Will we be seeing you around again?"

"I'm sure you will." Morgan put his hat on and strolled away, heading for one of the other wagons.

Neither Cody nor Angela said anything for a moment. The Ranger finally broke the silence by commenting, "Sort of duded up for a wagon-train journey, isn't he?"

Angela shrugged. "He's originally from Philadelphia. I don't imagine he considers himself dressed up."

"He give you any trouble?"

"Not at all. He was a perfect gentleman." Again, Angela didn't mention the blatant flirting Willard Morgan had engaged in while they were walking back to camp. She changed the subject by saying, "I wondered where you were when I woke up."

"Hope you didn't worry too much. I took a turn around the camp, just seeing if anything unusual was going on while most folks were asleep." Cody grimaced slightly. "Everything was as peaceful as could be, though."

"You would have rather it hadn't been?"

"The sooner we get what we came for, the better." Cody stepped closer to her and put a hand on her arm. His rugged face softened slightly. "How are you this morning?"

She knew he was referring to her mental and emotional states as well as physical, and she was well aware of what had prompted the question. Smiling up at him, she replied, "I'm fine, Sam. I'm just fine."

He bent and brushed his lips across her. "Glad to hear it. Angela . . ."

"There's no need to say anything else," she told him quickly. "We've been married for almost a year, remember? We should certainly be comfortable around each other by now."

Cody grinned. "I reckon you're right." His hand tightened on her arm for a second; then he released her with a light pat. "Well, since you've already fetched the water, I suppose I should rustle us up some breakfast. I make a pretty good stack of flapjacks, if I do say so myself. And Stone'll be ready to pull out before you know it."

"Breakfast is the wife's job"—she grinned at him— "but I guess we could make an exception this time."

Cody started to whistle as he began preparing the meal. Angela thought it was a good sound.

They had finished breakfast and Angela was putting everything away when Meg Duncan came over to the wagon. Angela greeted the widow warmly and Cody gave her a pleasant nod. Meg smiled and said, "Do you think you young people could put up with an old woman's company today? One of the Owens boys wants to drive my wagon, and I told him he could. You know how youngsters are; he thinks wrestling a bunch of stubborn mules'll be an adventure." She laughed. "But I've a feeling I'd be listening to a whole lick of cussing when he discovers just how stubborn those animals are, so I'd much prefer hearing your talk to his."

"We'd be glad to have you ride along with us," Angela told her. "Wouldn't we, Sam?"

"Sure," Cody replied, and Angela thought he sounded sincere. "You're welcome to join us, Mrs. Duncan."

"Only if you call me Meg," she said.

"All right. But you've got to stop referring to yourself as old," Angela said. "You're really not."

"Texas ages a woman," Meg said with a sigh.

"You've heard the old saying: 'Texas is wonderful for men and dogs but hell on women and horses.'"

Cody chuckled. "Whoever came up with that one just didn't know the right horses . . . or the right women."

Meg beamed, and Angela knew that Cody's veiled compliment had been appreciated. Angela said, "There's plenty of room in the wagon. Why don't you get up here behind the seat? I'm sure we'll be rolling soon."

"Oh, I'm sure of it, too," Meg agreed as she climbed agilely to the wagon box and stepped over the seat. "Caleb Stone's not the kind to waste daylight. In all the years I've known him, it's always been a struggle to get the man to pass an idle moment. He has to be busy with something all the time."

Cody's interest perked up at Meg's comment. Angela could see it on his face, even though he quickly concealed it. Meg didn't seem to have noticed. Cody helped Angela onto the seat and then climbed up beside her, taking the reins.

Caleb Stone rode by a few minutes later on his Appaloosa, calling, "We'll be movin' out in five minutes! All wagons to their places!" He went through the camp repeating his message, and the wagons began to roll out onto the road, forming an irregular line. The gaps filled in quickly as the last vehicles left the encampment.

Peering ahead from their position at the end of the train, Cody watched the wagon master for a moment, then asked their visitor, "You say you've known Mr. Stone for a long time, Mrs. Duncan?"

"I told you to call me Meg, because I intend to call you Sam."

Cody grinned. "Sorry, Meg."

"Well, to answer your question, I reckon I've known Caleb longer than anybody else I ever knew—except my late husband and my children. He and my Homer were good friends, you know. That's one reason I wanted to join this wagon train."

Cody and Angela both turned to look at her. Angela said, "Your husband and Mr. Stone were friends?"

"That's what I said, isn't it? Oh, I know what you're thinking. You've heard all those stories about Caleb being some sort of outlaw back during the war for the Confederacy. But he wasn't really, and neither was Homer. They were just trying to help folks."

Cody and Angela exchanged a glance. So Homer Duncan had been a smuggler along with Caleb Stone. That was interesting information. Angela wondered just how much Meg knew about those days, and she knew Cody was probably thinking the same thing. The most important question, though, was how much did the older woman know about Stone's current activities?

Angela was about to continue the probing when Cody's hand, ostensibly moving the reins, brushed against her knee. He shook his head slightly, just enough so that she could catch the gesture, indicating that he didn't want her to keep questioning Meg about Stone. He probably didn't want the woman wondering why they were so curious about the wagon master. It'd be better to proceed slowly so that Meg wouldn't be as likely to say something to Stone about all the questions they were asking.

Cody turned the talk in other directions. Meg spoke of her childhood in East Texas, her marriage at an early age to Homer Duncan, the hardships the young couple had faced. It was a story filled with suffering and tragedy, but Meg didn't dwell on those aspects. There had been happy, glorious times along the way, too, and that was what she seemed to remember most clearly. Not that she wanted to dwell on the past, either, Angela noticed. In fact, Meg frequently turned the conversation back to the present.

"I saw the two of you talking to that Mr. Morgan before we pulled out," Meg said around midmorning. "What did you think of him?"

"He seemed nice enough," Angela replied. "He wanted to help out, so I let him carry the canteens from the creek back to the wagon."

Cody just grunted noncommittally.

"A man like that needs a wife of his own," Meg said with a slight edge to her voice, "so's he'll quit paying so much attention to other men's wives."

Cody looked over his shoulder at her, his eyebrows drawing down in a frown. "What're you saying?"

"I'm saying he's a mite too attentive to gals that are already spoken for. Not that he doesn't pay attention to the unmarried ones, too. I reckon he don't much care either way. At least, that's the way it seemed while the wagon train was getting together back in San Antonio."

Angela met Cody's eyes squarely as he looked over at her. "You didn't tell me Morgan was flirting with you this morning," he said flatly.

She shrugged. "He's harmless, Sam. I've seen plenty of men like him. There didn't seem to be any point in causing trouble."

Suddenly she hoped that her nonchalant attitude and the comment about knowing other men like Morgan hadn't seemed too out of place, coming from the woman she was supposed to be. But if Meg thought anything about it, she didn't say so.

"I'm still going to keep my eye on him from now on," Cody said, and Angela felt a twinge inside her. Was he jealous? Knowing the truth about her and the men she had known—what he thought was the truth, anyway—how could he feel that way? Or had last night changed things between them even more than either one of them had suspected at the time?

Cody didn't say anything else about Morgan, and after a few more minutes of idle talk he rolled his shoulders in an effort to ease some of the aching muscles. Meg noticed the gesture and said, "You're not used to sitting on a wagon seat all day, are you, Sam?"

"Not hardly," he replied with a grin. "It's a heap different from riding on a horse."

"Well, you've got a fine mount tied on back behind the wagon. Why don't you let that dun stretch his legs a bit?"

"I've got to handle the mules—"

"I told you yesterday, Sam," Angela broke in, "I'm perfectly capable of handling the team. You saw as much when you finally let me drive for a while."

He nodded. "I reckon that's true enough."

"And Meg's here in case of any trouble." The idea was beginning to appeal to Angela now. If Cody rode ahead on the dun, it'd give her a chance for some private conversation with the older woman. Meg might be more likely to talk about Caleb Stone if Cody wasn't around. Angela persisted. "You go ahead. We'll be fine."

Cody hauled back on the reins, slowing the mules to a stop. "You ladies have convinced me. Just let me get my saddle out of the back."

He dropped down from the box and went around to the rear of the wagon. As he unloaded his saddle and began to put it on the dun, Angela watched the other wagons pulling away and remembered Stone's warning not to get too far behind. They were probably still too close to San Antonio to have to worry much about Indians, but every passing mile took them closer to territory that would be more dangerous.

Cody swung into the saddle and rode up alongside the box as Angela took the reins and got the mules moving again with a couple of cracks of the whip. "I'll ride with you until you catch up to the others," he said, obviously remembering Stone's words of warning just as Angela had.

It didn't take long to close the gap between them and the next wagon, not with the slow pace of the train. Once Angela had their prairie schooner back in position, Cody said, "I'll be back in a little while," then waved and urged the horse into a ground-eating trot. Angela watched him ride toward the front of the train and smiled at his obvious enjoyment.

Meg Duncan stepped over the back of the seat and

settled down beside Angela. "Now that Sam's gone, I reckon we can have us some woman talk," she said. "He's a good husband, is he?"

Angela nodded and said sincerely, "Yes, he is. One of the best."

God, it felt good to have a horse under him again! Even though it had only been a couple of days since he had ridden the dun, it seemed longer. Cody held the horse down, even though he sensed it wanted to gallop.

Stone was riding off on the left flank of the train, about a fourth of its length back from the lead wagon. Five other scouts worked for him, and they ranged around the train at intervals, a couple of men always riding a mile or so ahead to keep their eyes open for trouble. From what Cody had seen so far of the way Stone was handling the train, the wagon master was doing a good, efficient job.

Veering the dun to the left, Cody rode toward Stone, who must have heard him coming, because he twisted in his saddle and looked over his shoulder. As Cody rode up, he lifted a hand in greeting.

"Howdy, Cole. What're you doin' up here?"

"My wife ran me off," Cody replied with a grin. "Actually, Mrs. Duncan is riding with us today, and I think she and Angela wanted to talk."

"Yep, Meg's a great one for talkin', all right. Don't reckon you'd know it, but me an' her husband was friends and rode together back in the old days. Homer never had a whole hell of a lot to say, but when he did talk, it'd pay you to listen. Him and Meg was a good match for each other."

"It sounds like it." Cody patted the dun on the shoulder. "When she suggested I let this big fella stretch his legs for a while, I thought it sounded like a good idea."

Stone laughed. "Yeah, and it gives you a chance to rest your butt for a while if you ain't used to ridin' a wagon. Which I ain't and never will be. Don't see how you pilgrims do it, but I reckon I'm glad you do, else I wouldn't have a job."

"I don't think I'll ever get used to it," Cody said, shaking his head.

The wagon master, his eyes narrowing shrewdly, looked over at Cody. "You know, that's a mighty fine hoss you got, Cole—especially for a farmer. And you don't sit a saddle like a man who spends most of his time behind a plow."

Cody shrugged. "Just because I'm a farmer now doesn't mean I always was."

"True enough. Most fellas've been more than one thing in their lives." Stone leaned over and spat into the dust. "I ain't always been a wagon master, neither. Reckon you may have heard about that, happen you've been around this part of Texas for a while."

Cody found himself grinning. There was no point in denying his knowledge of Stone's past. He said, "I've heard a few stories. Most of them about how you kept people from starving and provided enough guns and ammunition so that the Comanches didn't drive the settlers all the way back to the Gulf."

"Well, I seen folks hurtin' because of the Yankee blockade who didn't have one damn thing to do with that war back East. Didn't seem right they should suffer 'cause some dadblasted politicians let their wranglin' get out of hand. So I done what I could to help out and make some money for myself at the same time." Stone sighed. "Them days're long gone, and I'm mighty glad of it. I'm gettin' old, and leadin' these wagon trains to California is about all I can handle."

The responsibilities of the wagon master's job would be too much for most men to handle, Cody thought, no matter what age they were. Caleb Stone was said to be as tough as whang leather, and Cody didn't doubt it for an instant. He felt an instinctive liking for the old frontiersman. The thought that Stone might be involved in smuggling those stolen rifles to the Comanches disturbed the Ranger. It didn't seem to be something that someone like Stone would do. As the man had admitted, he'd always been on the lookout for a way to make a dollar, but he'd also been concerned with the safety of the frontier's settlers. Selling guns to the Indians would fly in the face of everything Stone had always stood for.

But every man had his price, or so Cody had been told. He wondered what Caleb Stone's price was.

"You look like you done wandered off on me, boy," Stone remarked. "Must be mighty weighty thoughts goin' through your head."

"Just looking at the country," Cody said with a smile.

"Not much to look at, is it? Ever been through this way before?"

Just a few days ago, Cody thought, when he was riding in from Del Rio. But he said, "I've passed through it a time or two, back before I was married." That was the truth—in a way.

"Want to give that dun of yours a workout?"

"What'd you have in mind?"

"I need to ride ahead and relieve one of the advance scouts," Stone explained. "If you think your missus will be all right, why don't you come with me?"

Cody didn't have to think over the offer for long before nodding. "I'm sure Angela will be fine. Mrs. Duncan is with her, and she seems pretty unflappable."

Stone gave a hoot of laughter. "That's the damn truth!"

"And Angela can take care of herself, too." Cody hoped he was right. He'd never seen her handle any trouble except in the Crystal Slipper, where she was on her home ground. How she'd react to a dangerous situation out here on the trail was anybody's guess, but Cody had a feeling she'd do all right.

Stone heeled the Appaloosa into a faster gait, and Cody urged the dun on, staying abreast of the wagon master. The lead wagons of the train soon fell behind them as they rode over the rolling, brush-dotted hills. It took them about ten minutes to catch up to the advance scout.

"You can head on back to the wagons, Williams," Stone called out. "We'll take over now."

"Sure, boss," the scout replied as he wheeled his horse and rode back toward the wagon train.

When he was alone again with Stone, Cody asked, "Are you expecting any trouble?"

"Not really, but it always pays to keep your eyes open. There's still some bands of Comanch' around who like to stir things up, and out here there's always a chance of runnin' into some owlhoots who figure a wagon train to be easy pickin's. We're close enough to the border, too, that bandidos sometimes come across the Rio and raise hell. Yep, a man never knows what he'll run into 'round these parts."

Stone wasn't telling Cody anything he didn't already know. The Ranger was probably more aware of the dangers in this area than the wagon master himself, but it wouldn't hurt to let Stone think that he was little better than a novice. If the the man *was* mixed up in any wrongdoing, it'd be easier to catch him if he didn't consider Cody a threat.

They rode along side by side for almost an hour. Stone's usually taciturn nature relaxed considerably out here away from the wagon train, and he spun several yarns about the days during the Civil War, when he'd been a smuggler. Before that he'd been an Indian fighter and established one of the first ranches west of the Brazos. Cody found himself enjoying the tales and liking this man even more. Stone was a survivor of an earlier, even wilder era, a contemporary of men like Bigfoot Wallace, Ben McCulloch, Jack Hayes, and Jake Cutter. It'd be hard to arrest him if he turned out to be part of the gang that had stolen those Winchesters.

Stone abruptly reined in a bit, his eyes narrowing as he peered into the distance ahead. "Hold on there, Sam," he said. "Riders comin', and I can't tell right off who they are. Don't much like the looks of 'em, though."

Both men slowed their horses to a walk. Cody's keen

vision had spotted the approaching horsemen at the same time as Stone, but he didn't say so. As the on-coming riders closed the gap, Cody could make out their high-crowned, broad-brimmed headgear. Mexican sombreros, he thought. And the riders were well armed, fairly bristling with rifles, pistols, and knives.

Cody and Stone reined their mounts to a halt when fifty yards separated them from the other men. Quietly, Cody asked his companion, "Some of those bandidos you were talking about earlier?"

"Damn sure looks like it," Stone replied grimly. "Just sit your hoss and follow my lead, son. Maybe we'll get out of this alive."

The Mexicans rode on until the gap was only some thirty feet, then pulled their horses to a stop when one of the men held up his hand. They'd been coming fairly fast, kicking up a cloud of dust in the process. As it blew between the two groups and then slowly settled, Cody leaned forward in the saddle, resting his hands, right over left on the pommel. This was a damn serious situation. There were five of the Mexicans, and not a one looked as though he had an ounce of friendliness in him.

The bearded man who'd signaled his companions to stop slowly lowered his hand and glared across the intervening space at Cody and Stone. In accented English, he called, "You are a long way from anywhere, señores. What are you doing out here?"

"Just passin' through," Stone said casually. Cody knew he wasn't about to reveal the existence of the wagon train a mile behind them. Five bandits probably wouldn't bother such a large, well-armed group—but there was always a chance they just might be crazy enough to try something.

"We, too, are passing through, as you say. Perhaps we should all go on our way in peace, no?"

"Sounds like a good idea to me."

For the first time something resembling a smile appeared on the Mexican's face. "Before we go, we would like to know your name, señor."

"I'm Caleb Stone," the wagon master said firmly.

The Mexican's eyes narrowed slightly. "Caleb Stone. I have heard of you, señor. You have killed some of my people."

"That's true," Stone admitted. "But I've ridden with a heap of 'em, too. Some of the finest people I've ever known." His voice hardened. "Only ones I've ever done for were scum like you."

As the harsh words came out of Stone's mouth, Cody saw the same thing the wagon master had obviously noticed: Two of the bandits who were slightly behind the others were reaching for their guns. A showdown was coming, regardless of what he and Stone said or did.

"Scum?" echoed the bandit leader, looking surprised to hear the defiant comment. His hand darted toward the pistol tucked into the bright red sash around his waist as he howled, "Kill them!"

Cody drew and fired while the Mexican was still shouting, going for one of the men who already had a gun out. The explosions blended together, but the bandit's bullet screamed past Cody's head while the Ranger's slug punched through the man's chest. The Mexican went over backward out of his saddle.

Beside Cody, Stone also had his pistol drawn. The gun roared twice and the other bandit who'd been pulling his gun spilled off his horse, his weapon unfired. But by now the three remaining Mexicans, including the leader, had their own revolvers out and spitting flame and lead at the Texans.

There was no art or science to a gun battle like this, Cody knew. All you could do was stand your ground, try to keep a cool head, pick your targets, and hope the other son of a bitch was unluckier than you were. Slugs whined around and over his head as he cocked and fired, cocked and fired. The dun moved under him a bit, spooked slightly by the noise, but not much. The bandits' mounts were more nervous; they danced around, kicking up dust and making their riders poorer targets. Through the haze of dust and gun smoke Cody saw another bandit go down, whether from his bullet or Stone's he couldn't tell. Cody shifted the barrel of his gun and squeezed the trigger again. The leader of the bandits let out a shriek of pain and dropped his gun as he clutched a bullet-shattered elbow. Cody tried to locate the last man through the dust and smoke. He saw a flicker of movement, fired, and then the bandit suddenly loomed up close in front of him, charging forward with a mad cry of anger and hatred.

Cody jerked the dun to one side, but he was too late. The Mexican's horse slammed into the shoulder of Cody's mount, staggering both man and horse. The dun started to fall. Cody kicked his feet free of the stirrups and leapt clear, but no sooner had his boots hit the ground than something crashed into his back, and a heavy weight knocked him to the ground. The bandit had flung himself from his own saddle and tackled the Ranger. Cody twisted, lashing out with the barrel of his gun toward the man's head. The blow missed, and Cody saw the flicker of sunlight on an upraised knife blade.

The sharp crack of a rifle sounded before the knife could fall. A small black hole appeared in the bandit's forehead as his head jerked back on his shoulders. He tumbled lifelessly off Cody, who rolled away from the corpse and came up nimbly on his feet. His gun was still in his hand, and he had one bullet in the chamber. He looked around for somebody to use it on.

"Might as well holster it, son," Caleb Stone said as he put his rifle back in the saddle boot. "This little fandango's over."

All five of the Mexicans were down, Cody saw. Four of them were dead and the fifth soon would be. The leader of the bandits, who'd been disarmed by one of Cody's shots, was then finished off by Stone. The man was sprawled in the dirt with a huge red stain on the front of his grimy white shirt.

Cody reloaded the Colt, then slid it into its holster. He glanced at the body of the man who had almost knifed him. From the looks of things, Stone had emptied his Remington, then brought out the rifle to fell the last bandit—just in time to keep the man from killing Cody. The Ranger looked up at Stone, nodded, and said, "Thanks."

"Hell, you'd've done the same. Best mount your hoss. We got to get back to the train and swing it north a ways. Don't want the womenfolk and the kids to see this."

Cody moved to the dun, which had scrambled up and was standing nearby, unhurt from the fall it had taken. The Ranger was grateful for that, too. As he swung up into the saddle, he asked, "You plan to leave the bodies here, do you?"

"Ain't in much of a mood to bury 'em. There's buzzards and coyotes to take care of that sort of thing. Let's catch their hosses and get movin'. We got work to do."

Cody nodded. Stone was right. The wagon master had also saved his life. Cody was starting to hope he was wrong about Caleb Stone. . . .

CHAPTER
||||||||||||||||||||||||||| **9** |||||||||||||||||||||||||||

"**Y**ou handled yourself pretty good back there, son," Stone said as he and Cody rode back toward the wagon train. "And that dun of yours acted like he was used to gunplay." The wagon master squinted over at Cody. "What'd you say you did 'fore you started farmin'?"

"Didn't say," Cody replied curtly.

"Yep, that's what I thought. Well, I don't reckon you can hold a fella's past against him. Somebody like me ought to know that better'n anybody. You did plumb fine when the chips were down, and that's what counts."

Neither of them said much more as they rode at a good pace toward the wagon train. They had just topped a small rise and spotted the prairie schooners up ahead when they also saw a small band of men galloping toward them. A couple of the scouts were in the lead, accompanied by a half dozen men from the train, all of them carrying rifles.

The group reined in as Cody and Stone rode up to them. "Are you all right, Caleb?" called one of the scouts. "We heard some shootin'!"

"Everything's fine, Del," Stone assured the man. "You need to go back and start the train swingin' a bit north. Cole and me run into some owlhoots from the other side of the border, and I don't reckon what's left'd make a pretty sight for the women and kids."

The scout nodded in understanding and didn't seem

surprised that the two men had disposed of a whole band of Mexican bandits. He motioned for the men with him to turn around, and they rode back to the wagon train while Cody and Stone followed along at a more leisurely pace.

"They'll let everybody know we're all right," Stone said. "Imagine that wife of yours was a mite worried about you, Sam."

"She might not even have known I was with you," Cody said. But Angela would have probably figured it out when word passed through the train that Stone and one of the settlers had ridden ahead into some kind of trouble. She could have guessed that he would be sticking close to the wagon master.

By the time they reached the wagon train, the lead vehicles were veering slightly to the north. Cody lifted a hand in farewell to Stone, then galloped along the line of wagons till he reached the end. As he'd expected, Angela was waiting for him with an anxious expression on her face, and Meg Duncan looked concerned, too.

"Sam!" Angela exclaimed. "We heard you were mixed up in some trouble. Are you all right?"

"I'm fine," he said, turning the dun so that he could ride alongside the wagon box. "Stone and I ran into some bandits. They weren't after the train, probably didn't even know it was here, but they thought they could rob and kill a couple of travelers easy enough."

Meg laughed. "Reckon they found out different. Should've had more sense than to go after an old he-bear like Caleb."

Cody said, "We had more'n our share of luck, so we managed to down all of them. That's why the train's heading slightly north now; Stone wanted to give the bodies a wide berth."

He saw a shudder run through Angela. This kind of life was vastly different from the one she knew back in San Antonio. She said, "As long as you're not hurt, that's what matters."

Leaning over in the saddle, Cody squeezed her shoulder, and she reached up to pat his hand.

"Reckon I'd better get back to my own wagon," Meg said. "You young folks'd probably like to be alone for a while."

Angela said quickly, "No, Meg, that's all right."

But the older woman shook her head. "Didn't mean to come and roost all day," she said. "Besides, I'd better see how that boy's doin' with my wagon."

They were moving slowly enough that she was able to step down from the box without Angela having to stop the team. With a wave and a cheerful smile, she set out at a fast walk that would take her to her own wagon, some four or five vehicles on up the line.

Cody stayed in the saddle, content to ride alongside their wagon for the moment. Angela asked, "Are you really all right?"

"Not even a scratch," he told her. "It was mighty chancy there for a while, though. Five against two is pretty bad odds. But Stone's a slicker gunhand than you'd think from looking at him. He shot two of those hombres out of the saddle, then downed another one with his rifle—just as the fella was about to carve open my gullet with a knife."

Angela shuddered again, and Cody wondered if he should have left out the details of the brief fight. To get her mind off it, he went on hurriedly, "What did you and Meg talk about while I was gone?" He grinned. "Discussed husbands, I'd wager."

"You'd win." Angela summoned a smile, though she was still a little pale. "Meg talked more about her life with Homer. I managed not to be too specific when she asked about you and me. And she admitted something about Caleb Stone."

Cody tensed. "Something tying him to the gun smugglers?"

Angela smiled again and shook her head. "I'm afraid nothing of the kind. Meg's going to try to talk him into staying in California when the wagon train reaches the end of its journey. She's hoping he'll settle down with her."

"She wants to marry Stone?" Cody asked in surprise.

"And why not? They're old friends, and they have a lot in common. More than you and I do, probably."

Cody shrugged. "It's just that it's hard to imagine Stone settled down with anybody, even Meg. A man like that usually isn't happy unless he's free and out on the trail somewhere."

"Like you?" Angela asked quietly.

Cody didn't answer for a moment. Then he said, "I don't know."

After that both of them were silent for quite a while.

The noon stop was at Hondo Creek. By nightfall the wagon train should reach the town of Hondo itself, Cody calculated while he watered the horse and mules. As Meg Duncan had predicted, Caleb Stone rode along the length of the caravan advising the settlers that they wouldn't be stopped long enough to build fires and cook a meal. As soon as the animals had drunk enough and the water barrels and canteens had been refilled, the train would be pushing on.

When he led his dun and mules to the creek, Cody found himself beside the Easterner, Willard Morgan. Morgan and another man were taking a team down to the water. Smiling at the Ranger in greeting, Morgan said, "Hello there, Mr. Cole. I heard about your adventure this morning."

"Wasn't what I'd call an adventure," Cody said, not trying to match Morgan's friendliness. "Stone and I damn near got ourselves killed."

"Yes, but you didn't. And I've always heard that danger can be quite exhilarating."

"Wouldn't know about that. Generally when somebody shoots at me, the only things I feel are scared and mad."

Morgan nodded. "I know I would be. Scared, that is." He gestured toward the man with him. "By the way, this is my assistant, Jasper Mertz. I hired Jasper to help me with this trip to California. He handles most of the driving."

It came as no surprise to the Ranger that Morgan did little of his own driving. Cody barely glanced at the other man. Mertz wasn't an unusual sort. He was a chunky man in worn range clothes and several days' worth of beard stubble. He grunted an acknowledgment of the introduction, which Cody returned with a nod.

This was Cody's first chance to take a look at Morgan's wagon. It was an even more impressive vehicle than the one he and Angela had purchased from Hudnall's Wagonyard back in San Antonio. Constructed of the finest wood, iron, and canvas, the Easterner's wagon had a very solid look to it. The sideboards were higher than normal, too, Cody noticed. He frowned slightly. Sideboards like that could mean that the wagon had a false bottom—just the sort of place stolen Winchesters might be concealed.

Along with the wagons belonging to Josiah Croft and his group, he wanted to take a better look at Morgan's vehicle, Cody decided. That would have to wait for nightfall, though. He couldn't very well go poking around in broad daylight.

Stone called for everyone to get back in line, and less than ten minutes later the wagon train was rolling again. Cody tied the dun to the back of the wagon and reclaimed the reins of the mule team from Angela. She protested that she was fine, but he thought she looked tired. "You've done your share," he assured her. "Break out some of those leftover biscuits and some jerky, and we'll have lunch."

It was simple fare and not very appetizing, but it kept both of them going through the long, hot afternoon. The train passed through the small settlement of Hondo late that day and camped on the western edge of the community. Anyone who wanted to replenish their provisions had a chance to do so now, but Cody and Angela didn't need anything, and he decided to pass on the opportunity. They were getting closer to

his usual stomping grounds, and it was possible he
might run into somebody in town who'd recognize him
as a Ranger. From here on out he intended to stick
close to the wagons whenever they were near a settlement.

Meg Duncan joined them for supper, carrying with
her a can of peaches she'd brought from San Antonio.
Cody grinned when he saw the airtight. Nothing tasted
better at the end of a hot day than peaches.

Over supper Meg commented, "Sam, you're takin'
that gunfight mighty casual. Most men would be more
frazzled if they'd nearly got themselves shot less'n
twelve hours earlier."

Cody shrugged. "It's all over. Don't see any point in
worrying about it now."

"Well, that's an unusual way of looking at things, I
got to say."

Maybe she was right, and he should have made more
out of the encounter with the bandits, Cody thought.
He'd been a little shaky at the time, but the feeling had
passed. As a Ranger he ran into violence pretty often,
and he supposed he was getting used to it. Cody
frowned slightly. He wasn't sure if he liked that idea or
not.

After supper Meg excused herself. "I need to have a
few words with Mr. Stone," she said, trying to sound
businesslike. But Cody knew from the glance she exchanged with Angela that business wasn't really what
was on Meg Duncan's mind. He grinned to himself.
Stone might have faced a lot of danger in his time, but
now he was up against a menace unlike any other he
had known—a woman with marriage on her mind.

Best keep such comments to himself, Cody decided
with a chuckle.

When Meg had gone, Angela moved closer to him.
She was sitting on the ground, her legs drawn up so
that she could hug her knees. Resting her chin on
them, she asked quietly, "What are you going to do
now?"

Cody sipped from his cup of coffee and answered in

equally soft tones, "Thought I'd try to get a look in some of the wagons tonight. I'll wait till everybody's turned in."

"Make sure everyone's asleep."

"It'll be late enough so that everybody will be, except the sentries that Stone posts at night. And they'll be far enough out from the camp that they shouldn't notice what I'm doing. Stone's more worried about threats from outside than inside."

"Do you still think he has something to do with the rifles?"

Cody didn't answer for a moment, but the furrows in his brow deepened. Then he said, "I don't want to think so. He strikes me as a man who'll do to ride the river with. But it's my job to suspect everybody."

"Even me?" Her voice was teasing.

Cody took a deep breath. "Even you," he said solemnly, and he saw the shock in her eyes when she realized he wasn't joking.

"You really mean it, don't you?" she asked, staring at him.

"I didn't say I still suspect you. But back in San Antonio I didn't know what your game was. I still don't, but if you were working with the gun smugglers, you've had plenty of chances to kill me before now." He was glad he had decided on the spur of the moment to get this out into the open. It had been eating at him for too long. "I've decided I'm going to trust you."

She didn't say anything, and she jerked her eyes away from his. He could tell she was angry. Maybe she had a right to be.

After several moments of silence, she glanced at him again. "I suppose you do have to look at things that way," she said, and while her voice was still somewhat stiff, he thought her anger had eased. She went on, "I swear, Sam, I'm not working against you. I thought surely you'd know that by now."

"I said I trusted you."

"Yes. I know you did." Angela sighed. "I suppose we'd better start getting ready for bed."

She stood up and went to the wagon, climbing onto the lowered tailgate and disappearing inside. Cody sat by the fire, slightly upset with himself for angering her but also glad he had finally voiced some of the things that had been preying on his mind.

The fire was dying down when he finished his coffee and got to his feet. He walked to the back of the wagon and asked, "Are you still awake?"

Angela's voice came to him out of the shadows. "Yes."

"You want me to sleep under the wagon tonight?"

"We've had this discussion before, Sam. You're my husband. You belong in here."

He hoisted himself up, and after raising the gate and lowering the canvas flap he crawled over to the bunk. A little moonlight filtered into the interior of the prairie schooner, but not much. Not much light was required, though. Her hands brushed his body, found his shoulders, and pulled him down to her. Cody was surprised at her eagerness. His mouth found hers, warm and waiting, in the darkness.

Suddenly something hard prodded him in the side as he embraced her. He stiffened as she hissed, "Do you know what that is?"

"Reckon it's probably a gun," he said coolly.

"No, you damned fool, it's a pot handle!" Angela laughed as she took the item away from his body and pressed it into his hand. She was telling the truth, all right, Cody realized, a bit disgusted with himself.

"Now," she went on, "are you going to believe me when I say that I'm not working with that gang of thieves?"

Cody had to chuckle to himself as he realized the ludicrousness of the entire situation. "I suppose I'd better believe you," he said. "Else you're liable to take that pot after me."

"That's right. Now, kiss me again."

Cody tossed the pot aside and did as she told him. Several times, in fact.

• • •

Later, as Angela was nestled against his side, she kicked one leg free from the lightweight blanket they'd pulled over themselves and raised the long, smooth limb into the air. "Look familiar?" she asked Cody.

"A mite. I reckon I must've seen it before. Maybe even kissed it a time or two."

She giggled. "No, silly. Remember the sign over the door of the Crystal Slipper?" She bent the leg at the knee.

The filtered moonlight was sufficient for Cody to make out the sensuous shape of her leg and imagine it clad in black lace and a crystal slipper. "You were the model for the sign?" he asked.

"That's right."

"Well, you couldn't have picked a better one."

She kissed his bare shoulder and let her fingertips play among the brown hairs on his chest. "Thank you, sir. My, aren't you gallant?"

"What I am"—Cody regretfully took her wrist to keep her hand from straying lower—"is an hombre who hates the fact that he's got to get back to work."

Instantly, Angela became more serious. "Do you think it's late enough?"

"I reckon. I haven't heard anybody stirring around outside for a while. Of course, part of the time I probably wasn't listening too close. . . . Anyway, I ought to check."

He sat up, reluctant to leave the warmth of her arms. His shirt was somewhere nearby, and after groping around for a moment he found it. In a matter of seconds he had shrugged into the garment, pulled his pants on, and located his boots. With them in his hand he went to the rear of the wagon and leaned out to study the stars in the sky.

"After midnight," he whispered. Angela was sitting up now, the blanket wrapped around her. Cody went on, "I'll be back in a little while."

"Be careful, Sam," she told him, tension edging into her voice.

"Don't worry. I'll be back before you know it."

Cody stuffed his feet into the boots, then picked up his gun belt and dropped out of the wagon. The camp was quiet around him. All the fires were down to glowing embers, but between them and the moon and stars, there was enough light for the Ranger to see the other wagons, their canvas coverings rising as light-colored bulks in the shadows. Cody buckled the gun belt around his waist and slipped silently away from his wagon.

Earlier, he'd tried to fix in his mind the location of Willard Morgan's wagon, and he also had a pretty good idea where to find the prairie schooners belonging to Josiah Croft and his friends. Morgan's was closer, as were a couple of other wagons belonging to single men the Ranger wanted to check. He hoped that he wasn't suspicious of Morgan simply because he disliked the man. But Croft was still his leading suspect.

Cody catfooted around some of the cooking fires and approached one of the other wagons he had seen with high sideboards. As he drew nearer he could hear loud snores coming from inside. The occupant, a man whose name Cody didn't know yet, was obviously sound asleep. The Ranger paused at the rear of the wagon. There was no canvas flap hanging down inside, so he had a clear view over the gate. He could see the shape where the snores originated. The man was lying in the middle of the wagon, his belongings piled around him. Carefully, Cody reached inside.

His searching fingers found the bottom of the wagon bed. He estimated how far down it was, then leaned back to compare it to the sideboard. Frowning, Cody decided that if the vehicle did indeed have a false bottom, the space it concealed would have to be extremely narrow. He could eliminate this one; it wasn't carrying the stolen Winchesters. Cody hadn't expected to hit the jackpot on the first crack, but he still felt disappointed.

Willard Morgan's wagon was next on his mental list. He headed toward the fancy rig. So far his movements around the camp hadn't disturbed the mules or the

horses or even the dogs. He couldn't count on that
luck lasting forever.

When he reached Morgan's wagon, he paused outside it as he had at the other vehicle, listening closely.
He heard the telltale sounds of two occupants: one
man snoring, although not as loudly as in the first
wagon Cody had visited, and the deep, regular breathing of another man. With Morgan and Mertz both ac-
counted for, Cody repeated the same test he had used
before. He reached inside and found the wagon bed,
gauging its depth against the depth of the sideboard.

Again he reached the same conclusion—there was
no false bottom in Willard Morgan's wagon. In a way
Cody was glad. He didn't like to think that his percep-
tions as a lawman could be colored too much by his
personal feelings. Morgan would do well to steer clear
of him—and especially well away from Angela—but if
he and Cody ever clashed, it would be as man to man,
rather than as Ranger and outlaw.

That left one other wagon, then those belonging to
Croft and his partners.

Cody moved away from Morgan's wagon, skirting
another couple of vehicles. He had his eyes fixed on
the next one he intended to investigate, but his senses
were alert enough to pick up the faint, sudden scuff of
sound from a booted foot. Cody started to whirl
around.

He heard something whipping through the air, and
then it crashed against his head. In that splintered instant of time that had been all the warning he had, he'd
tried to duck out of the way of the blow. As it was,
whatever hit him glanced off the side of his head,
rather than smashing directly against his skull. Even
the grazing blow was enough to set off fireworks in his
brain and send him staggering to one side. His balance
deserted him, and he fell.

Trying to fight off the agony in his head, Cody rolled
onto his back, caught a glimpse of a dark shape looming over him, and desperately kept rolling. The club in
his attacker's hand came down against the ground

where the Ranger's head had been a split second before. Cody tried to launch a kick at the man, but his muscles didn't seem to be working right. The kick was feeble and wide of the mark.

He scrambled up on hands and knees and dived forward as his opponent straightened up again from the blow that had missed. Cody caught the man around the knees, staggering him but not knocking him off his feet. The club came down on Cody's back, sending more waves of pain through him.

Cody groped for the gun in his holster, not wanting to rouse the camp with a shot but not wanting to lie there and get beaten to death, either—which was exactly what would happen if he didn't turn the odds back in his favor fast. But his fingers found only an empty holster. During the rolling and diving, the Colt had fallen from its sheath, no doubt lying on the ground nearby now. Cody probably could have found it, if he'd had the time, but the other man wasn't going to give him that chance. He'd have Cody's brain smashed to a bloody gray mess in a matter of moments.

"Hold on there! What are you doing?"

A voice that was somehow familiar shouted the words. Cody heard a rush of feet. The figure looming over him suddenly dropped the cudgel and turned to run. Cody would have tried to stop him, but he was too dizzy and sick with pain from the blow to his head.

A couple of men ran past him, and then seconds later strong hands grasped his arms and lifted him to his feet. He winced as the light from a lantern struck his eyes like a fist. The man carrying the lantern exclaimed, "Dear God! Are you all right, brother?"

"Croft . . . ?" Cody muttered, finally recognizing the voice. "Is that you?"

"That's right, Mr. Cole. What happened? You look like you ran into a tree."

"More like a tree ran into me," Cody groaned as he lifted a hand to his head. The men on either side of him were still holding him up, so he thought he could chance the movement. The fingers came away wet and sticky with blood. His tongue a little thick, he went on, "I reckon if you look around, you'll find a length of wood with some blood and hair on it. Somebody jumped me and tried to knock my brains out with it."

"Do you think the man was trying to rob you?"

Cody tried to shake his head but quickly gave that up as a bad idea. "Don't know. I was just heading into the brush to relieve myself." Even groggy, his mind was still working enough to come up with a story to explain why he was wandering around the camp in the middle of the night. He went on, "Reckon that had to be it. The goddamn bastard wanted to rob me."

"Now, there's no call for talk like that," Croft said, his voice stern. The reaction puzzled Cody. Most men who'd just been hit over the head with a club would probably cuss a bit, too.

Things became clearer a moment later, however, as two men came out of the brush and said to Croft, "He got away, Reverend. We couldn't see hide nor hair of him in the dark."

Reverend? Croft was a preacher? That explained his comment about Cody's profanity, but it sure muddled up the Ranger's suspicions of him.

"Could've been just a drifter," Croft remarked. "I'd hate to think anyone belonging to the wagon train could do such a thing." He stepped to one side and gestured to the men who were supporting Cody. "Take Mr. Cole back to our wagons. That head of his will need some looking at."

Cody tried to protest, but he was still too dazed and weak for his efforts to do any good. The commotion had roused several other people in the camp, and as Croft and his companions helped Cody over to their wagons, the minister assured everyone who asked that the trouble was over.

Angela had probably heard the shouting, too, and she'd be worried. Cody said, "My wife . . ."

"I'll send someone to fetch her. Don't worry, Mr. Cole, everything will be fine."

Cody wanted to believe that. Croft's deep, authoritative voice should have been reassuring.

By the time they reached the preacher's wagons, Caleb Stone was waiting there. "Lordy, Sam, what happened to you?" he asked in surprise when he saw the blood on Cody's head. The wagon master glanced at Croft and muttered, "Sorry, Josiah."

"That's all right, Caleb. I realize you're agitated." Croft set the lantern down on the lowered rear tailgate of one of the vehicles. "Mr. Cole was attacked by someone. Probably a drifting thief. I think he'll be all right, if we can get that cut cleaned up."

Somebody placed a wooden crate on the ground as a seat, and Cody sank gratefully onto it. Stone came closer and looked at the gash left by the club. The wagon master grunted. "Nasty wallop," he said. "You got any whiskey, Josiah?"

"Yes. Strictly for medicinal purposes, like this." Croft rummaged in the wagon and produced a bottle.

Cody knew this was going to hurt.

Stone wet a rag with the whiskey and began cleaning away the blood. The Ranger winced at the stinging effect of the alcohol. As Stone was swabbing at the wound, Angela rushed up, wearing a robe and accompanied by one of Josiah Croft's companions.

"Sam!" she cried. "This man came to the wagon and said you were hurt—"

"I'm all right, Angela," he told her. "It's not as bad as it looks."

He wasn't sure of that yet, but Stone confirmed it a second later. "A fella's head always bleeds like a stuck hog when it gets cut open, Mrs. Cole. Look here, you can see for yourself that your husband's injury don't look near as bad, once you clean all the blood off it. Shoot, I don't reckon it'll even leave much of a scar." He began wrapping a strip of clean cloth around the Ranger's head to keep the wound covered.

"You're right, I suppose," Angela admitted but obviously still somewhat agitated. "Who would do such a thing?"

"A robber is what we suspect," Croft said. He held out his hand. "I don't think we've met, ma'am. I'm the Reverend Josiah Croft, and these men are friends of mine who have agreed to help me in some missionary work."

The ache in Cody's head had eased a little now that Stone had finished the bandaging. Looking up at Croft, the Ranger echoed, "Missionary work?"

"Yes, indeed." Croft smiled broadly. "I think I told you earlier that I move around a great deal in my profession, Mr. Cole. Look at that crate you're sitting on."

Cody stiffened as he glanced down at the crate. It was long and fairly narrow, about the right shape to hold a dozen Winchesters. . . .

Josiah Croft gestured into the interior of the wagon. "We've got ten of these crates in each wagon, including that one you're sitting on. We're going to deliver them to people who most desperately need them."

Cody stood up slowly, aware that Angela was watching him intently. "You've got false bottoms in your wagons," he said to Croft.

"Of course. That makes carrying our precious cargo much easier." Croft bent, grasped the lid of the crate on which Cody had been sitting, lifted it, and reached inside. "Here. Even if you already have one, Mr. Cole, an extra can always come in handy."

Smiling, the minister withdrew his hand and pressed a thick book bound in black leather into Cody's hands. It was a Bible.

CHAPTER
||||||||||||||||||||||| **10** |||||||||||||||||||||||

"And you thought he was a gun smuggler."

Cody leaned back against the pile of goods that Angela had arranged inside the wagon to make a seat for him. With a sour expression on his face, he responded testily, "I didn't notice you taking up for him until tonight."

"Well . . . maybe not," Angela said. "But I didn't have any idea he was a preacher, either."

Cody had felt foolish plenty of times in his thirty-odd years, but seldom had he felt as ridiculous as he had when Josiah Croft revealed what he was hauling in the false bottoms of his wagons. The minister and his followers were on their way to California to distribute Bibles to the poor—a far cry from selling stolen Winchesters to the Comanches.

The Ranger lifted a hand to rub his eyes. His head still hurt from the whack it had taken earlier, and his back was stiff and sore, too. By morning, he'd have a couple of pretty good bruises, he supposed. He'd talked Croft into letting him take a couple of slugs from that whiskey bottle—strictly for medicinal purposes, of course—and he felt a little better now. But the question of who had tried to kill him was still nagging at him.

And he had no doubt that was what the attacker had had in mind. At first he'd thought that maybe the man just wanted to scare him off. For a few minutes he'd even considered Reverend Croft's theory that the shadowy figure had intended to rob him. But all Cody's instincts told him that the attacker had wanted him dead, pure and simple.

"Somebody on this train knows I'm a Ranger," he said, breaking the silence that had fallen between them.

Angela blinked in surprise. "But that's impossible. The only people who know are—" Her jaw tightened and her eyes began to blaze with fury. "You're saying you don't trust me anymore." Her voice was flat, hard.

Cody shook his head. "That's not what I'm saying at all. Could be somebody on the train had seen me before and just now remembered who I am. Or maybe they overheard you and me talking and added things up when they found me snooping around the camp in the middle of the night. Hell, maybe they *don't* know I'm a Ranger. Maybe they just didn't want anybody stumbling onto what they're doing."

Looking relieved and a little less angry, Angela said, "I suppose you're right. That means we're going to have to be more careful from now on, doesn't it?"

"Damn right. If they're suspicious of me, they're probably suspicious of you, too."

"Don't worry about me. Let's just do our job."

Cody felt like asking her when she had been sworn in as a Ranger, but he suppressed the urge. No need to get her mad at him again, he decided.

"We'll keep our eyes open," he said. "Reckon tomorrow's soon enough to start, though. Stone said I needed some rest after that clout on the head."

"Yes, I heard him. He said for you to take it easy." Angela slipped the robe off. Cody saw by the moonlight that she was nude underneath it. She snuggled closer to him.

"I'm not sure that's what Stone meant," he said after a momentary pause.

"Don't worry. I'll do all the work."

Cody didn't feel like arguing.

• • •

Caleb Stone rode back along the line of prairie schooners the next morning and swung his horse to jog alongside Cody and Angela's wagon. "How're you feelin' today?" he asked the Ranger.

"Not bad," Cody replied. "I've got a headache and my back's sore, but neither of them is bothering me much. You did a good job patching me up, Caleb." He poked a thumb toward his head. "I can even wear my hat."

"Glad to hear it. You come mighty close to gettin' your skull split open, from the looks of it. Got any idea who'd want to do such a thing?"

The question was casual; Cody knew Stone's interest was anything but. Even if the man wasn't mixed up with the stolen rifles, as wagon master he'd want to know whatever was going on that involved his train.

Cody shook his head carefully and lied, "I have no idea."

He had ideas, all right; he just couldn't put names and faces with them yet. But he was more convinced than ever now that the Winchesters were hidden somewhere in this group of wagons. His hunch back in San Antonio had been correct.

Stone leaned forward in the saddle and asked Angela, "Is this stubborn man of yours telling the truth, ma'am? Did he rest all right last night?"

She smiled at Cody, then answered the wagon master's question. "He rested just fine, Mr. Stone."

"Well, that's good. Feel up to doin' a little outridin' with me again today, Sam?"

Cody wasn't sure he was feeling that chipper, but he sensed that Stone wanted to talk to him in the privacy of the wide open spaces. He nodded again and said, "Reckon that'd be okay, if Angela doesn't mind handling the team."

"I don't mind at all," she said. "I know how much you like to ride that horse of yours."

Cody grinned. "I'll catch up to you in a few minutes, Caleb."

"That'll be fine." Stone waved and heeled his horse into a trot, moving up alongside the other wagons.

As soon as Stone had left, the smile dropped off Cody's face and he said seriously, "You keep your eyes open while I'm gone. My Winchester's right behind the seat, and it's loaded. Can you handle a rifle?"

"I used to know a man who always said, 'I can make it dance,' when somebody asked him that question. I'm not that good, but I've used a rifle before. I'll be all right, Sam."

"I wouldn't be going with Stone except I've got a hunch he wants to talk to me about last night."

"Well, you'd better get moving if you're going to catch up to him."

Cody nodded and handed her the reins. He stepped down from the box, went around to the back of the wagon, and reached inside for his saddle.

Five minutes later he rode up to the front of the train, passing the lead wagon and spotting Caleb Stone about a quarter of a mile ahead. The wagon master was moving at a deliberate pace, and it didn't take Cody's dun long to close the distance between them. Stone looked around as Cody rode up. He said, "Glad you came out here, son. I reckon it's time you and me had us a talk."

"What about?" Cody asked, sure that he already knew the answer.

"About who the hell you really are," Stone replied, giving Cody a hard look from the corner of his eyes. "You show up at the last minute as we're pullin' out of San Antone, claimin' to be a farmer. But you ride a hoss that's used to gunfire, and you handle a Colt about as slick as anybody I ever saw. You ain't no sodbuster, Sam. Ain't now, an' never have been. Then last night somebody tries to kill you. I figger you're bound to know why."

When Stone fell silent, Cody waited a few seconds, then asked, "Is that all you've got to say?"

"I reckon it's enough. I'm responsible for the safety

of all these people, mister. I got a right to know what's goin' on."

For a moment Cody considered taking out his watch and showing Stone the Ranger badge concealed inside the timepiece. All his instincts told him that Stone was on the level and could be trusted. But he left the circled star where it was, unwilling to reveal his true identity just yet. Instead, he said, "You're right, Caleb. I'm no farmer. I joined this train because I'm looking for somebody."

Stone gestured toward the bandage that was still wrapped around Cody's head. "Reckon they found you first."

"That's what it looks like."

"You got trouble with the law? You goin' after somebody who double-crossed you?"

Cody shook his head. "I give you my word the law's not after me, Caleb. And I can't tell you who I'm looking for."

For a long moment Stone didn't say anything, and Cody could tell that the wagon master was mulling over what he had just heard. Finally, Stone said, "I'll take the word of any man who stands up to trouble like you did yesterday, son. But I don't like bein' in the dark about this other business. Still, I reckon you got your reasons."

"That's right, I do." Cody glanced around. The two of them had ridden out a considerable distance from the train. Glancing back, he could barely see the wagons a half mile or so behind them. Again he thought about telling Stone that he was a Ranger—

The glint of sunlight on metal came from a ridge about two hundred yards to their right. Cody caught just a glimpse of it, but that was enough. His brain screaming a warning at him, he left the saddle in a dive, crashing into Caleb Stone and knocking the wagon master off his horse. Both men sprawled to the ground.

Cody heard a thud and then the whine of a spent slug ricocheting off something. Stone yelled, "What the hell!" Cody rolled over, leapt to his feet, and grabbed for the trailing reins of the dun.

"Get your horse down!" he called to Stone.

The wagon master followed his lead, scrambling to his feet, clutching the bridle of his Appaloosa, and pulling the spotted horse down onto its side. Cody already had the dun on the ground. Another bullet kicked up dust a few feet to the side. Cody dropped behind his horse, using the animal for cover. He hoped the dun wouldn't catch a slug; the ugly mud-colored horse might not be pretty, but it was smart and had plenty of grit.

Cody's Winchester was back at the wagon, but Stone had his long gun with him. He reached over the quivering flank of his mount and pulled the Winchester from the boot. Levering a shell into the chamber, he lined the sights on the distant ridge. "Shots come from up there?" he called to Cody.

"That's where I saw the sun flash."

Stone nodded, laid his cheek against the smooth wooden stock of the rifle, and fired. The Appaloosa in front of him jumped a little, but not much. Stone's mount was obviously accustomed to loud noises, too.

Cody raised his head slightly as Stone fired twice more. He couldn't see where the bullets hit, but he hadn't heard any return fire from the ridge. Two shots had come from the bushwhacker, and so far that was all. Stone's rifle fell silent. After a moment, he asked, "You reckon that scared him off?"

"Don't know," Cody replied. "But I wouldn't go to moving around too soon if I were you."

"Wasn't plannin' to, son," Stone said dryly. "Wasn't plannin' to at all."

The two men stayed where they were in the meager shelter of their horses for several minutes before they chanced getting to their feet. No more shots came from the ridge. Keeping the horses between them and the site where the ambusher had waited, they let the animals stand again. Stone pointed toward his saddle. "Lookee there. That first bullet glanced off the horn right after you knocked me out of the saddle," he said. "Knew it hit somethin' from the sound."

Cody glanced at the damaged saddle, then looked back toward the ridge, figuring the angles. He'd been riding to Stone's right, between the wagon master and the ridge. If he remembered right, he'd been just slightly ahead, too, maybe four or five inches. If he hadn't jumped when he did, he realized, that first slug would have torn right through his body.

Whoever had been lying in wait up there was a damn good shot.

"We'd better get back to the wagons," Cody said, "before that son of a bitch doubles back and tries again."

Stone was already swinging up into his saddle. "Damn right. Come on."

They rode east at a gallop, the prairie schooners coming closer and closer. Once again the scouts came out to meet them. One of them gibed, "You'd better stop ridin' ahead, Caleb! Somebody's always takin' shots at you!"

"As long as they keep missin'," Stone grunted. "You boys get back to your places. All the excitement's over."

Another ambush was unlikely now, Cody thought as he and Stone rode slowly back along the train. Stone asked, "You reckon that fella was after you or me?"

"I'd say me. I was more in line with those shots than you were."

"That's the way it looked to me, too. You still want to keep them secrets under your hat, Sam? Might get you killed . . . and maybe I could help you with whatever it is you're doin'."

"Thanks anyway, Caleb," Cody said sincerely. "I reckon I'd better play out the hand myself, though."

Stone shrugged. "It's your hide we're talkin' about, son—and that pretty woman of yours."

He had a point, Cody thought. Somebody was on to him, that much was obvious. If anything happened to him, he felt certain Stone would take care of Angela, and Meg Duncan would be on her side, too. He'd have to talk it over with Angela, but he decided that if anything *did* happen, she ought to tell Stone what was really going on and leave the matter in his hands.

She was perched on the edge of the wagon seat, leaning forward anxiously as she kept a tight grip on the reins. The lines of concern on her face eased as Cody and Stone came within earshot. "I heard shooting again, Sam," she called. "Are you all right?"

"Just fine," Cody told her. In truth, the excitement had started his head hurting again, and diving off the horse hadn't done much for his sore back. But he'd be all right, he assured himself. "Any trouble here?"

Angela shook her head. "None at all."

"I'd best be gettin' back to the front of the train," Stone said. "You take it easy, now, Sam."

Cody nodded and rode beside the wagon, watching Stone make his way back to the lead. Angela asked, "What happened?"

"Some bushwhacker took a potshot at me from a ridge," Cody said. "Came close to hitting me. Stone, too."

"Then that clears Mr. Stone, doesn't it? Surely if he's working with the smugglers, they wouldn't have tried to ambush you with him right there. The shot might have hit him instead."

"I thought of that," Cody admitted. "And I reckon Stone's not much of a suspect anymore. But I can't ignore the possibility completely. He could be playing a mighty deep game."

"And a dangerous one," Angela pointed out.

Cody inclined his head in agreement.

He frowned as he considered everything that'd happened. After a few moments, he said, "I don't know about you, Angela, but I'm getting a mite tired of this."

"I am, too, but what can we do about it?"

"I think it's time we set a little trap."

Now she was the one frowning. "What kind of trap?"

"Whoever's got those rifles doesn't want me poking

around the train. I'd wager they're keeping an eye on you, too. That's what's going to play into our hands. You're the key to it."

"Me?"

"That's right, Angela," Cody said. "You're the bait."

He hated the idea of deliberately putting her at risk, but they were both in danger as long as the gun smugglers remained free—as were the peaceful settlers on the frontier who'd have to take the brunt of Indian attacks if the Comanches got their hands on those rifles. Still, by the time he'd explained to Angela what his idea was, he had just about talked himself out of going through with it. She was the one who insisted on proceeding with the plan.

"I'll be close by, so don't worry," Cody told her over supper, wondering just whom he was trying to reassure, Angela or himself. "I never got around to searching that other wagon—or Croft's, either—before that fella waylaid me in the dark. With the preacher eliminated that just leaves us with one likely suspect."

Cody had done some asking around about that man. His name was Hendrickson, a Swede, and he was traveling alone. Supposedly he had a family up near La Grange and planned to send for them once he got established in California. That might be true, but it might also be a phony story concocted to explain why he was by himself.

"If Hendrickson is part of the gun smuggling plot, he's not in it by himself," Cody went on. "He was driving his wagon today when somebody took that shot at me. But from what I've seen of him on this trip, I never figured him for the brains of the operation, anyway. Somebody else is running things, and I don't like the idea that they may be pulling *our* strings, too."

Since he'd thought it over, he realized that Willard Morgan could still be involved. Morgan could be the ringleader, the man operating in the shadows whom no one knew.

"So," Angela said, cradling a cup of coffee in her hands, "I'm to wait until everyone is asleep, as you did last night, and then search Hendrickson's wagon."

"Just try to see if it's got a false bottom. If it does, it could be the one we want. He'd be hard-pressed to carry all those rifles in one vehicle, but I suppose it could be done. Wheels don't leave much of a mark on this hard ground, so I couldn't tell from his tracks if he's carrying a heavy load or not."

Angela looked down at the coffee cup. "Maybe we'll find out tonight."

She was nervous. Despite her claims to the contrary, Cody could tell that she was worried about carrying out her part in the plan. He reached over to her, rubbed her shoulder and the back of her neck. She closed her eyes and leaned forward, making a little moan of plea- sure. They were sitting on a log in front of the fire, and she slid closer to him. Cody slipped his arm around her shoulders.

"You know," he said, "I've enjoyed being married to you. And I don't just mean—"

"I know what you mean," she broke in. "You're talking about the closeness, the shared purpose, the quiet times and the talking." She looked up at him, her beautiful face solemn. "Did you ever think of getting married, Sam? For real, I mean?"

Cody took a deep breath. "I reckon every man's thought of it now and then. But as long as I'm in the line of work I'm in, I don't have a whole hell of a lot to offer a woman. The pay's not very good, I have to move around pretty often, and I'm never at home. Seems like there's always some job that needs doing somewhere else—and a man like me never knows when he's going to play out his string." He shook his head. "Nope, it wouldn't be much of a life for a woman."

She rested her head on his shoulder and sighed. "No, I suppose not."

He thought she sounded sadder than he had ever heard her.

When he had taken care of cleaning up after their meal, he joined her in the wagon. She was still dressed, and Cody knew she wasn't in the mood for any love-making tonight. They sat quietly together, going over the details of the plan several more times in low voices. Time dragged, but eventually the camp settled down. Cody finally checked to make sure all was quiet, then came back to her and nodded.

"I'll go first," he said. "Let me slip out, then give me fifteen minutes to get into position. You head over there then."

"I understand," Angela said, her voice sharp with tension.

Cody wasn't wearing his hat tonight, and instead of his high boots with the silver spurs, a pair of soft leather moccasins covered his feet. He tucked the sheathed Bowie knife behind his belt, leaving the holstered Colt and cartridge belt behind. The success or failure of his plan depended more on stealth than anything else.

He had parked the wagon so that the front of it was in the deep shadow of a large tree. Moving cautiously, he slipped out of the vehicle, stepping over the seat and lowering himself to the ground. The previous night he'd left from the back, as Angela would in a few minutes. Cody went down into a crouch and crawled under the wagon, using the big wheels for cover as he edged his way to the opposite side and emerged behind a small clump of brush.

The next few minutes were long ones as Cody worked his way from bush to tree to patch of shadow. He covered most of the distance on hands and knees, some of it on his belly. When he finally reached a tree that would give him a view of the Hendrickson wagon, he cautiously stood and leaned against the trunk, flattening himself as much as possible.

A cool breeze touched his brow as he waited. The long, hot, dry spell still hadn't broken, but there was a hint of something in the air tonight. It reminded him of the night back in San Antonio when he had trailed the

Grady brothers to the Alamo. Storms might be prowling the area tonight.

Surely fifteen minutes had passed by now, Cody thought. Angela would be quiet as she approached the wagon, but she wouldn't be taking the pains that he had to work himself into this spot. It would take her only a few minutes to reach Hendrickson's prairie schooner. She should be showing up at any second now. . . .

He saw a flitting shadow behind the wagon and knew Angela had arrived. Barely daring to breathe, Cody watched her come closer to the vehicle, slipping up to the rear gate. He forced his eyes off her and concentrated his attention on the area around and behind her. If someone had been keeping an eye on their wagon—and he was betting that somebody had been—they'd have seen her leave and would be wondering where she was going. Wondering enough to trail her, Cody hoped.

Sure enough, there was more movement in the darkness on the other side of the Hendrickson wagon. Cody slipped the Bowie out of its sheath as the gliding shape resolved itself into a human figure. The Ranger was about twenty feet from Angela, maybe thirty from the man stalking her. If he had to, he could throw the big blade that far with reasonable accuracy. He didn't plan to interfere unless it was absolutely necessary, though. If the other watcher didn't bother Angela, Cody might even be able to trail him back to wherever he had come from.

Keeping his gaze fastened on the man in the shadows, Cody waited while Angela reached into the wagon without disturbing the sleeping Hendrickson. It didn't take her long to determine what she wanted to know, because after only a moment, she turned and started to walk quietly away from the vehicle. Cody tensed as she passed the patch of shadow where the other man was lurking.

Suddenly the watcher lunged forward, clamping a hand over Angela's mouth and wrapping his other arm around her waist. Cody darted out of his hiding place,

pulse hammering in his head from anger and fear for
Angela's safety, and raced toward the two struggling
figures. Angela might have been trying to cry for help,
but the hand over her mouth completely muffled any
sound she was making.

Cody covered the ground in a hurry. Angela's resis-
tance must have kept the other man from noticing his
approach, because Cody was able to rush right up to
him. The Ranger dived, crashing into Angela's captor.
All three of them spilled off their feet.

Cody came up first, lashing out with a foot. It caught
the man in the stomach and he fell back. Cody came
down hard on his foe's chest, using his knees to pin the
man down and drive the air from his lungs.

Grabbing the man's hair, Cody jerked his head back
and put the blade against his throat. "You'd better quit
wiggling around like that," Cody warned in a low
voice, "or you'll slice your own gullet open, mister."

The man stopped thrashing. Without taking his attention off his prisoner, Cody called softly, "Angela!
Are you all right?"

"I'm fine, Sam. What . . . what's happening?"

"I'd say we just caught us a thief and a gun smuggler," Cody grated.

The captive spoke up then. "You . . . you damned
fool!" he whispered harshly, straining to get the words
out without moving his throat too much, the cold edge
of the Bowie a constant reminder of just how close he
was to death. He went on, "Papers . . . in my coat
pocket!"

There was something familiar about the voice, but
Cody didn't place it right away. Wary of a trick, he said
to Angela, "This fella's saying something about some
papers. See if you can find them." To the prisoner, he
added, "And if you try anything, you bastard, you'll be
dead quicker'n you know it."

Coming closer, Angela knelt beside the man,
reached into his coat, and after a moment's fumbling
around located a thin sheaf of papers. As she withdrew

them, Cody saw that they had been folded and tied together with a thin string.

"Those will . . . tell you . . . who I really am," the man croaked.

"Strike a match," Cody instructed Angela. "I don't like drawing that much attention to ourselves, but I'm curious enough to want to know what he's talking about."

He knew she had matches in one of the pockets of her dress. She found one and felt around until she located a rock on which she could strike it. "Here goes," she whispered.

The rasp of the lucifer sounded louder than it really was. Cody squinted against the sudden glare, and he was able to see the reddish light wash over the face of the man beneath him. He was not at all surprised to see the handsome features of Willard Morgan.

"You played it a bit too fancy, Morgan," Cody growled. "Reckon we'll know what your game is pretty soon now."

A little smile tugged at Morgan's mouth. Given the position the man was in, such smugness was infuriating, Cody thought, but he bit back his anger. There were more important things to tend to now than taking this arrogant Easterner down a peg or two.

"Oh, my God!" Angela Halliday exclaimed quietly as she looked at the unfolded papers in her hand.

Cody frowned at the shock he heard in her voice. "What is it?" he demanded, letting up on the pressure of the knife against the prisoner's throat.

Before she could answer, Morgan's smile widened into a grin and he said, "I imagine this so-called wife of yours just discovered that I'm a major in the United States Army, an investigator attached to the office of the provost marshal. I'm looking for those stolen Winchesters the same as you are, Ranger. So get off me, you goddamned oaf!"

CHAPTER
‖‖‖‖‖‖‖‖‖‖‖‖‖ **11** ‖‖‖‖‖‖‖‖‖‖‖‖‖‖

Cody didn't know which surprised him more—the fact that Morgan was an army agent or that the Easterner knew he was a Ranger. Without looking around or easing up on the knife, Cody asked over his shoulder, "Is he telling the truth, Angela?"

"These papers identify him as Major Willard Morgan, all right," she replied somewhat shakily. "I think you'd better let him up, Sam."

Cody didn't budge. "How do we know he's the real Major Morgan?"

"You idiot," Morgan said coolly. "The army doesn't hand out identification papers to just anyone who asks for them. Of course I'm who I say I am!"

"You talk mighty big for a man with a knife at his throat, mister." Cody considered the matter for a few seconds, then pulled the blade away and stood up. "Of course, most army officers I've run across have been too big for their britches. Reckon that makes me believe you as much as those papers do."

Morgan sat up and touched his throat, then looked at his fingers. Finding no blood, he got to his feet. "You know, you almost got yourself into a great deal of trouble, my friend," he said.

"I'm not your friend," Cody snapped. "You'd best tell me what the hell's going on here, before I reconsider and come after you with this Bowie again."

As he brushed himself off, Morgan stated, "I already told you, I'm looking for those rifles that were stolen from the supply depot. Now, before we announce all the other details of our mutual mission to everyone in camp, I suggest we adjourn to a more private setting."

"Reckon we need to palaver, all right," Cody muttered. He slipped the Bowie into its sheath but kept it handy. "Come on. We'll go back to my wagon."

None of them said anything as they made their way across the camp. When they reached the wagon, Angela climbed in first, followed by Morgan and then Cody last of all. His muscles were still tense with readiness in case Morgan tried something.

When they were all seated in the wagon bed, Angela lit a lantern and put it on top of a box of supplies. Cody told her, "Let me have those papers."

She handed the documents over, and a quick scan of their contents confirmed what Morgan had said: He was a U.S. Army major, attached to the provost marshal's office. With a frown, Cody gave the papers back to Morgan, who tucked them away in the same pocket.

"I'm glad you finally believe me," he said. "There's no reason why we should be working at cross-purposes. We all want to recover those rifles before the Comanches get them, don't we?"

"You're telling the story," Cody said noncommittally.

Morgan sighed. "I understand. You want to know just how much *I* know about this affair. Very well. I can tell you that upwards of two hundred Winchester repeating rifles were stolen from a supply depot in East Texas. The army was supposed to be testing the guns to see if they should consider replacing the regulation Springfields with them." The major's voice took on a grim tone. "Now it looks as though the Comanches will be doing the field testing."

"How did you know they were being smuggled west on this wagon train?" Angela asked, beating Cody to the question by a second.

"I didn't," Morgan said with a shake of his head. "To be completely honest, I still don't. But I'm not the only agent assigned to this case. The wagon train was a possible means of transporting the rifles to the Indians, so the provost marshal gave me the job of going along to see if I could find them. We had heard through some of our intelligence contacts that the Texas Rangers were looking for the guns, too, and when I saw you two join the wagon train at the last minute, I was a little suspicious of you. I'd say my suspicions have been confirmed. You are a Ranger, aren't you, Cole?"

Cody took a deep breath. "I am," he admitted. "Real name's Cody, front handle whittled down to Sam, just like we've been using."

"Well, then, does that explain everything to your satisfaction, Cody?"

The Ranger lifted a hand to the bandage around his head. "Not quite. Why the hell'd you try to beat me to death last night?"

"That wasn't me," Morgan said quickly. "And I don't know anything about it. It seems to me the most likely answer to that question is that the men smuggling the rifles stumbled onto your real identity, just as I did."

"What about those potshots at Stone and me earlier today?" Cody asked sharply.

Morgan shrugged and tried a not very convincing smile. "I'll own up to those. But I was just trying to scare you off, maybe make you think you should stop poking around as you've been. I know you have good intentions, but I don't need anyone interfering with my own investigation. However, I never intended to hurt anyone."

"Those bullets came mighty damn close," Cody remarked, trying to control his anger.

"I'm sorry. They *didn't* hit you, you know," Morgan pointed out.

Cody just grunted. He wasn't ready to accept the army man as an ally just yet. "What about tonight? Why'd you jump Angela like that?"

"I just wanted to talk to her, but I knew if I stepped out of the shadows and surprised her, she might let out a cry and wake up the camp." Morgan turned to Angela and said, "I'm sorry, my dear. I truly didn't mean to frighten you. I was going to explain who I was, but I didn't get the chance before your 'husband' came crashing into me."

"That's all right, Major," she said. "I guess we all just made some honest mistakes."

Cody wasn't ready to admit that quite yet. He still felt a strong, instinctive dislike for Willard Morgan. But if the man was telling the truth, there was no reason for them to continue working against each other.

"I suppose we did," Morgan said in reply to Angela's comment. "In fact, for a while I suspected that you and Sam here might be part of the gang that stole those guns." The major chuckled. "Of course, I can see now that such an idea is ludicrous."

Cody frowned. Something tickled at the back of his mind, something that wasn't quite right. But he wasn't sure what it was, and he found when he tried to concentrate on the feeling that whatever caused it had slipped away.

"What do we do now?" he asked.

"Well, I had intended to ask you to abandon your investigation and let the army handle matters," Morgan said. "Now I'm not so sure that's a good idea. In another few days the wagon train will be reaching Del Rio and then turning to follow the Rio Grande and the old Butterfield Stage route to El Paso. I was certain the rendezvous with the Indians would come before we reached Del Rio."

Cody nodded as he considered Morgan's theory. "Probably somewhere this side of Sycamore Creek. That's been my guess all along. It's rugged country, and there's not a whole hell of a lot out there."

"You sound like you know these parts," Morgan commented.

"Well enough. And I wonder whether the gang's going to deliver the rifles directly to the Indians."

Morgan looked confused. "Why, what else would they do?"

Cody frowned with annoyance. The army could have
sent somebody who knew something about these
things, he thought. "You ever hear of the comancheros?"

"They're outlaws of some sort, aren't they?"

"They see themselves more as traders, but who they
trade with puts them on the wrong side of the law,
that's for damn sure. They're white and Mexican renegades who deal directly with the Comanches. There
are comanchero strongholds scattered from the Rio
Grande to the Panhandle, and the Indians all know to
bring stolen horses and cattle to those camps. The comancheros take the stock and give the Indians white
man's goods in return, mostly old guns but also anything else that might strike an Indian's fancy—and that
could be damn near anything. The comancheros do a
little raiding themselves from time to time, but for the
most part they just deal with the Indians. They're
about the only ones who can do so safely. Anybody
else tries, the Comanch' usually just kill them and take
what they want."

The Ranger paused, shaking his head. "But like I
said, these gun smugglers might try to bypass the comancheros and sell the rifles directly to the Indians.
The payoff could be high enough to risk it. At first the
Comanche didn't set any store by gold or any other
kind of white man's money. Lately, though, they've
started to understand it. Rumor is there's a lot of loot
cached here and there in Indian camps."

Morgan nodded and said slowly, "I see your point.
Then there's a chance we'll have not only Indians but
also these comancheros to deal with."

"Yep. Unless we find those guns mighty fast."

"Then we'd better put all our information together,"
Morgan suggested. "Who are your suspects—other
than me, that is?"

Cody didn't return the self-assured grin that Morgan
gave him. He said, "Starting out, you and Josiah Croft
were the ones I was looking at. But Croft turned out to

be a preacher and you're a government man, so I guess I'm not much of an investigator."

"Don't sell yourself short. As for me, I have a sneaking suspicion our esteemed wagon master may know more than he's telling."

Cody shook his head. "If you're saying Stone's in on it, I've got a feeling you're wrong. I don't have any evidence to prove he's not guilty, but my hunch is he's as straight as can be now."

"He has a history of criminal activity," Morgan pointed out.

The Ranger shrugged. "Folks can change."

"I don't believe he's part of the gang, either," Angela put in.

Morgan just looked at her and smiled. Cody had noticed that Morgan didn't ask any questions about the true nature of their relationship. The major's mocking reference to Cody as Angela's husband had been his only comment on the matter. From the look Morgan was giving her now, he didn't take her seriously at all.

He might have cause to regret that, Cody thought with the first touch of amusement he had experienced tonight. If there was one thing he had learned during their brief association, it was that Angela Halliday was to be taken very seriously.

Morgan said, "We could go to Stone with my identification papers and your Ranger badge and reveal why we're really here. In fact, we could demand to search every wagon in the train. Stone couldn't very well refuse unless he's part of the gang. That would tell us which side he's on."

"Might get some innocent folks killed, too. Those gun smugglers would probably start throwing lead before we even got to them in our search." Cody shook his head. "I'm all for direct action, too, when the time comes. But I think we've got to play our cards close to the vest for a while longer."

"Don't wait too long," Morgan advised, "or it might be too late."

The man was probably right, Cody thought, but damned if he was going to admit it to him. "We'll all keep our eyes open and see if we can figure out where those Winchesters are. Then we'll move against whoever's got them, only quiet-like."

"Very well." Morgan moved to the rear of the wagon. He paused and looked back. "I assume I can count on your discretion?"

Cody nodded. "We'll keep quiet if you will."

"Then none of us has anything to worry about. Good night."

Morgan was wrong about that, Cody thought as the army agent disappeared into the shadows. They had plenty to worry about. If Morgan was telling the truth about not being involved in the attack on Cody the night before, that meant that someone else on the train knew the Ranger's true identity. And that someone was determined to stop him from accomplishing his goal.

Even if it meant killing him.

Cody didn't sleep much that night; his thoughts were full of everything that'd happened in the last week and a half. It seemed even longer than that since he'd left Del Rio for San Antonio. As he stared into the darkness with Angela slumbering somewhat restlessly beside him, he mused that every time he ran into a likely suspect, his suspicions wound up getting the hell shot out of them. Caleb Stone, once a smuggler, seemed to have reformed completely; Josiah Croft had turned out to be a preacher, a man of God; and Willard Morgan, despite being a nickel-plated son of a bitch as far as Cody was concerned, was an army officer working on the same case. Of all the people he had suspected of being involved with the theft of the rifles, only Angela was still a mystery to him.

Yet despite that, he trusted her more than any of the others.

Sometime far into the night Cody dozed off. He wasn't sure how long he had been asleep, but when something jarred him awake, a faint line of gray showed at the rear of the wagon where the canvas flap was pushed slightly aside. Dawn wasn't far off.

As Cody sat up sharply, he heard a shout, then the crash of gunfire. Mouthing a curse, he jerked his Colt from the rolled-up gun rig beside him and hurried to the back of the wagon bed, then shoved his head and shoulders past the canvas.

"Everybody out!" Caleb Stone's stentorian bellow rang across the camp. "We're under attack!"

That much was obvious, Cody thought. Pistols and rifles were cracking almost constantly now. Men shouted and women screamed. In the dim, hazy light Cody saw riders sweep by on the outside of the rough circle the wagons had been pulled into the night before.

Suddenly, Angela was at his side, a hand clutching his shoulder. "Indians?" she asked breathlessly.

Cody tossed a glance at her. Her hair was tousled, and her eyes were still filled with sleep. She was lovely no matter what the hour, he thought, a smile flickering fleetingly across his face. "No, comancheros, I think."

So far, all of the horses he had seen carrying the raiders were wearing saddles, and it was damned unusual to find Indians with gear like that. They preferred using just blankets to protect the backs of their mounts.

Angela frowned. "Why would comancheros be attacking the wagon train?" As she asked the question she flinched a couple of times when bullets whined past close enough for her and Cody to hear them.

"They know the guns are here," Cody said, putting the theory together even as he spoke. "And they know that the thieves plan to sell them directly to the Indians. The comancheros don't want that to happen, so they're trying to steal the rifles themselves."

Angela nodded. "That makes sense," she said.

Both of them were crouched low in the wagon, using

the sideboards for as much protection as possible.
Cody leaned back out again, Colt in hand, and fired at
one of the figures galloping by. It was hard to be sure
with so much dust and gun smoke in the air, but he
thought the comanchero went tumbling out of the saddle.

He turned and told Angela, "The Winchester behind
the seat—get it and use it! Anybody on horseback is
probably one of the comancheros." He felt safe in that
assumption. With a surprise attack like this, none of
the settlers would've had time to get mounted on their
saddle horses.

Angela crawled toward the front of the wagon as
Cody threw a few more shots at the attackers. He was
trying to draw a bead on one of the comancheros when
someone nearby yelled, "Look out, Sam!"

Cody jerked his head around in time to see that one
of the raiders had penetrated the circle and was about
to cut loose at him with a long-barreled revolver. But
before the man could pull the trigger, Caleb Stone appeared out of the dust and fired both charges from the
double-barreled shotgun in his hands. Both the comanchero and his mount went down, torn hideously by
the buckshot at that close range.

A few vehicles away another raider leapt his horse
over a wagon tongue and turned sharply toward Stone,
even as the wagon master gave Cody a grin and a small
wave. Cody saw the man coming and shouted, "Behind you, Caleb!" Stone wheeled as quickly as he
could, dropping the greener and grabbing at the Remington on his hip.

Cody fired first, the slug whipping over Stone's head
to drive into the chest of the onrushing comanchero.
As the man fell backward off the horse, the animal kept
coming straight toward Stone, never veering as the
wagon master tried to throw himself out of the way.
The horse's shoulder clipped Stone, spinning him
around and knocking him to the ground.

More and more of the comancheros were inside the
camp now, yelling and shooting. Stone tried to push

himself up, but the collision had stunned him, Cody saw, and he was shaking his head groggily. Cody jumped out of the wagon and ran to Stone's side as more of the attackers closed in. The Ranger fired the last two rounds in his pistol as he reached the wagon master. Going down on one knee, he smoothly tossed the empty Colt over to his left hand and used the right to snag the Remington in Stone's holster. He knelt there beside the stunned frontiersman, snapping off shots right and left. Two comancheros crashed to the earth not a dozen feet away.

"Sam!" Angela called from the wagon as she levered another round into the chamber of the Winchester. "Bring him over here!"

She gave them covering fire, the rifle cracking wickedly, while Cody grasped Stone's arm and hauled him to his feet. Together they ran awkwardly for the protection of the prairie schooner. Not that it offered much in the way of shelter, but it was better than being out in the open.

They were halfway there when Cody felt a blow like a giant fist smash into his left arm, just above the elbow. He grunted from the impact and stumbled, dropping the empty Colt he held in that hand, and now it was Stone who had to help him. There wasn't much pain, but Cody had been shot before. He knew the hurting would come later. Shaking his head, he regained his balance and hurried on to the wagon with Stone.

Angela let out a scream as they neared it. Fearing that she had been wounded, Cody pressed the Remington back into Stone's hand and lunged forward. His left arm hung limp and useless, but he was able to clumsily scramble into the wagon. "Angela!" he cried. "Are you all right?"

She had shrunk back away from the opening and was staring wide-eyed at him. Lifting a trembling finger, she pointed at the bloodstain on his shirt. "You're going to die!" she shrieked in a voice that shook with near hysteria. "I can't stand it . . . not again! I can't lose you, too!"

And then she began to cry, a soul-numbing wail that turned Cody cold inside. He grabbed her shoulder with his good hand and said sharply, "Angela, I'm all right! I'm all right! Stop it!"

Actually, he wasn't sure he was all right at all. There hadn't been time to check the wound. But as he glanced down at himself, he had a feeling it looked worse than it really was. The left side of his shirt was stained with blood, as if the bullet had torn through his torso in that spot, but he knew the gore had really come from his arm. The slug had ripped the fleshy inside part of his upper arm. He was fairly certain it had missed the bone, but the injury was still a mess.

Angela hadn't stopped crying. In fact, she was getting louder. Cody looked her over to be sure she wasn't injured, then clenched his jaw, not wanting to do what he was about to. But he slapped her anyway, hoping it would shock her out of her hysteria. The blow cracked against her cheek. She blinked several times, staring up at him with the red imprint of his hand on her face, then suddenly sagged against him, still crying. The sobs that wracked her were different now, and after a moment she straightened up and choked out, "Are you . . . are you really all right?"

"I will be," Cody assured her. Then he turned his head slightly, having become aware that the gunfire outside had died away somewhat.

A second later, though, Stone called from the rear of the wagon, "Here they come again! If the lady's all right, son, grab that repeater and rattle your hocks back here!"

Angela had dropped the Winchester on the floor of the wagon bed. It had been fully loaded when she started firing it, but Cody had no idea how many of the fifteen bullets were left in the magazine or if one was in the chamber. He held the barrel between his knees, worked the lever, picked up the unfired cartridge that was ejected, and stuck it in his shirt pocket. Then he hurried to the back of the wagon and knelt there, nodding at Stone, who was standing close by, thumbing shells into the Remington. Cody glanced around the camp and saw several dead comancheros but no live ones.

A fresh wave of gunfire came from the attackers as they charged again, seemingly determined to overrun the wagon train this time.

Cody and Stone snapped their weapons up and fired at the same instant, the Ranger handling the Winchester one-handed. All along the side of the circle facing the marauders guns roared as the settlers, many of them veterans of the Civil War, rose to the occasion and fired with cool, devastating accuracy. The hail of lead ripped into the comancheros.

Stone let out a rebel yell with the enthusiasm of a man half his age. "That'll show them bastards!" he shouted as he reached up to pound Cody on the back. A dozen or more of the raiders had flown out of their saddles at that volley from the wagon train, and the others were wildly wheeling their horses and had the animals digging dirt as fast as they could in the opposite direction.

Cody jacked another shell into the rifle's chamber and kept it lined on the fallen comancheros, just in case any of them wanted to get up and make a fight of it. But none of them were moving, and after a minute he decided they were all either dead or unconscious. He put the Winchester down and then grabbed the tailgate of the wagon as a sudden wave of dizziness washed over him.

"You all right, Sam?" Stone asked, looking up at him. "Hell, you caught a bullet! Never noticed till now. You'd best sit down."

Cody summoned up a grin. "Reckon I'll fall down instead, Caleb," he said.

He supposed that was exactly what he did next, but he wasn't sure, because he was out cold by the time he landed.

* * *

The first thing Cody saw when he woke up was Angela
Halliday's face. Normally, that would have been a
mighty pleasant experience, but not now. He hurt too
badly all over, and Angela looked too worried.

"You can stop frowning now," he told her in a raspy
whisper. "Reckon I'll live."

"Of course you will," she said, relief shining in her
eyes. "You're too stubborn to do anything else." She
feigned anger. "A bullet hole in you, and you keep
fighting just like nothing was wrong."

"Wasn't time to do anything else." Cody cast his
mind back over the events of the early morning and
found that his memory was remarkably clear. He recalled everything that had happened, from the first
alarm to the end of the battle with the comancheros.
Now, he realized as he looked up at the arching cover
of canvas, he was stretched out on the bunk inside the
wagon. His arm hurt like blazes, and his head was
throbbing. Still, there were things to do, so he shifted
slightly and tried to push himself into a sitting position.

Angela frowned again and put her hands on his
shoulders. "What do you think you're doing?" she
demanded, holding him down. "You've been hurt.
You've got to rest."

"I'll be all right," Cody told her through gritted
teeth. "I need to talk to Stone."

"He said to tell you he'll stop by later. Until then,
you're supposed to take it easy."

Cody shook his head, ignoring the ache in his skull.
"Too many people have been telling me that same
thing. There's work to do. We've got to find those rifles."

"Oh, damn the rifles!" Angela suddenly exploded.
"I wish I'd never gone to see Major Jones!"

Cody let himself sink back against the pillow she had
placed beneath his head. The time had finally arrived
for the truth to come out, he sensed. He said, "Why
did you go to the Rangers?"

"Because I felt it was my duty." She didn't look at

him as she explained, "My . . . husband . . . was a Ranger."

"Husband!" The exclamation jolted out of him.

She smiled faintly. "You didn't think I'd been a saloonkeeper all my life, did you? There was a time when I was a simple married lady. My husband's name was Jim Halliday. You may have heard of him." Her voice hardened. "He was killed helping to clean out a gang of rustlers up around Medina. People have started to call it the Lost Creek Fight."

Slowly, Cody nodded. "I remember," he said in a quiet voice. "I knew some Rangers got killed there. Didn't know your husband. I'm sorry."

"You should be. You would have liked him. The two of you"—her voice broke momentarily, but then she went on—"the two of you are a great deal alike. Both devoted to your jobs . . . and I guess some of that devotion rubbed off on me while I was married to Jim. When I heard about those rifles, I wanted to help. That was the first time since he . . . was killed . . . that I wanted to do anything for someone else."

"What about the Crystal Slipper?" Cody asked, knowing that she wanted to talk, painful though it might be. "How did you wind up there?"

"I inherited some money from an aunt just before Jim died. We talked about taking it and buying a ranch somewhere. Jim didn't want to resign from the Rangers just yet, though, so we put it off. After what happened at Lost Creek, I wanted to get as far away from the type of life we'd had together as I could. So I took the money and bought a saloon."

"And all the men?" Cody's voice was harsher than he had intended.

Angela smiled. "They were just . . . distractions, I guess you could say. When I was in bed with them, I concentrated on the physical pleasure and nothing else. It helped shut out the grief. But I never went with any of them more than once, because I was afraid I might start to care about someone if I did." A couple of tears rolled down her cheeks. "And then you came along, damn you. Right away you reminded me of Jim, and I was afraid it might be a mistake to choose you that night. But I talked myself into it anyway. Then, when I found out you were a Ranger, too—"

She broke off with a shake of her head, unable to continue. She didn't need to; Cody understood. That was why she'd turned so cool toward him when she saw the Ranger badge. She was trying to put up a wall so that she wouldn't be hurt again.

After a long moment, Angela swallowed, wiped the tears away, and said, "No matter how hard I tried, I couldn't stop what I was starting to feel for you, Sam. That's why I suggested that I pose as your wife and come along on this trip. That's why I made love to you. My heart was stronger than my head."

Cody reached over and caught her hand, squeezing her fingers tightly between his. He wasn't sure what to say. Maybe there wasn't anything that needed to be said right now.

They stayed there, holding hands, and the pain that was inside each of them eased a little.

CHAPTER
▌▌▌▌▌▌▌▌▌▌▌▌▌▌▌▌ 12 ▌▌▌▌▌▌▌▌▌▌▌▌▌▌▌▌

Angela sighed as she stepped down from the wagon. Cody had dozed off again, and she was glad. He needed his rest to recover from the loss of blood. Caleb Stone had cleaned and bandaged the wound while Cody was unconscious and assured Angela that, barring infection, it wasn't a serious injury.

The wagon train wasn't going to be moving today, Stone had decreed following the attack. They needed time to tend to the wounded—more than a dozen men—and bury the dead: three men and one woman. The slain comancheros had been dumped in a nearby wash until a decision could be reached about whether or not to bury them. Everyone seemed to be in agreement that the company had been very lucky not to suffer more losses than they had, but still a pall of sorrow and anger hung over the camp. It didn't help matters that none of the settlers knew why they had been attacked.

As she walked aimlessly around the camp, Angela thought about what she had told Sam Cody. Despite her best intentions, she had opened herself to him, revealing things she had sworn she'd always keep secret. Just as she'd feared, she had grown to care for him too much. The times when he'd been in danger during this trip had gnawed at her, and she had almost lost control a couple of times, especially the night when one of Croft's men had come to tell her that Cody was hurt. That had been the worst—until today.

She would never forget the sight of his stumbling toward the wagon, shirt stained and slick with blood. What she had seen at that moment had blurred with the memories of her husband, and she was screaming for both of them when Cody's slap finally brought her back to her senses. Now her emotions were all jumbled up inside her, and she couldn't figure out what she felt or thought. Somehow she had to sort out all the confusion.

She needed someone to talk to, she realized, someone with a sympathetic ear who might be able to help her make sense out of everything. She considered looking for Meg Duncan, but this problem might require more than a dose of Meg's homespun philosophies. Glancing around the camp, she spotted Willard Morgan standing over by his wagon, talking to Jasper Mertz. She shook her head; the army man was hardly the type she'd choose to unburden herself to.

Angela looked up and saw that she had wandered close to Josiah Croft's wagons. This was a stroke of luck. The minister might be just the one to help her with her problem. Preachers were used to such things, after all.

She didn't see Croft around either of his wagons, but he could be inside one of them, she reasoned. Gathering up her skirt—and her courage—she walked quickly toward Croft's prairie schooners, pausing at the rear of the first one she came to. She looked over the raised gate and called, "Reverend Croft?"

"What the hell!" The exclamation came from a man who had been crouching in the deep wagon bed. He almost fell over as he spun around to see who had spoken. In his hands he clutched a new Winchester rifle.

Angela saw the gun in the same instant she saw the section of false bottom that had been lifted from the wagon bed, revealing the contents of the well: a crate, its lid lifted and two layers of Bibles shoved aside, holding long, oilcloth-wrapped bundles that could contain only one thing. Time seemed frozen as Angela stared into the wagon. She was too shocked by the discovery she had just made to hear the footfalls behind her.

But then a hand came down on her shoulder, and the seconds began to race by again. She snapped her head around as the fingers tightened on her shoulder. Without looking at her, Josiah Croft stared angrily at the man in his wagon and said in a low, furious voice, "I told you to leave those rifles alone, Harley. We had enough guns to drive off those comancheros without breaking into the merchandise. But you had to get one of them out, didn't you?"

The man didn't answer. He stuffed the Winchester back into the crate as fast as he could and covered the bundles with Bibles again.

Angela's stunned mind told her to scream, to fight, to do *something*. But all she could manage was to stare at Croft and finally say, "You're not a preacher, are you?"

"I'm sorry you had to see this, Mrs. Cole. No, I'm not a minister, but I'm afraid you're going to need one—for your funeral."

Cody knew Angela had thought he was asleep when she slipped out of the wagon, but he was still awake. It was just easier on his head to lie back with his eyes closed while he tried to muddle his way through everything that had happened. He had no doubt that Angela had been telling the truth, for he'd finally seen behind all of her masks to the real woman.

But that didn't put him a single step closer to those stolen Winchesters.

His eyes flicked open at the sound of someone stepping to the rear of the wagon. "Sam?" Caleb Stone called softly. "You awake, son?"

"I'm awake, Caleb," Cody replied. "Come on in."

Stone pulled himself up and swung over the gate. "How're you feelin'?" he asked. "I saw your wife walkin' around and figured you might be asleep, but I thought I'd stop by and see."

"I'm all right." Cody got his right elbow under him and pushed himself up into a sitting position. He was shirtless, his left arm wrapped in bandages. Angela had rigged a sling out of a piece of one of her petticoats to keep the injured arm from moving around.

The wagon master chuckled humorlessly. "You're a mite bunged up, boy. Reckon if not for you, though, I'd be dead now. 'Pears I owe you my life."

"Nope." Cody shook his head. "Don't forget those bandidos. We're even, Caleb."

Stone hesitated, then nodded. "Even."

"You said you saw Angela outside?" Cody frowned slightly. He wondered what she was up to.

"Yep. She didn't notice me, though. From the looks of it, she had a mighty weighty problem on her mind. You and her havin' trouble?"

Cody didn't know how to answer that question. Instead, he asked, "Where was she going?"

"Looked like she was headin' toward Josiah Croft's wagon. Thought maybe she had somethin' to talk over with him."

"I don't know what it'd be," Cody said. He shrugged. Maybe Angela just needed to talk to somebody and thought the minister would be a good listener. Idly, Cody went on, "You and Croft're old friends, are you?"

Stone shook his head. "Never met the man until the train started formin' up in San Antone. Reckon he's just such a friendly cuss, you feel like you've knowed him for a long time." He hunkered next to the bunk, took a plug of chewing tobacco from a pocket of the buckskin shirt, and started to cut off a piece with his hunting knife. "Seems like a nice fella. He'd have to be a hell of a preacher to convert them hardcases he's got workin' for him."

"I thought they looked like sort of rough types for missionaries," Cody commented dryly.

"Oh, they been behavin' themselves, right enough. But I reckon they all went to see the elephant a few times 'fore they reformed." Stone put the chaw in his mouth and worked it to one side. "They can handle guns, too, lucky for us. I saw one of 'em fightin' off them comancheros with a brand-spankin'-new Winchester."

Cody's eyes narrowed abruptly. "A new Winchester?" he echoed.

Stone nodded. "'Course, I was a mite too busy to be studyin' on some other fella's gun, but it looked new to me. Like it'd never been out of the crate."

"Shit!"

Cody was off the bunk before he knew it, crouching and reaching for his holstered Colt. Somebody—Stone or Angela, most likely—had obviously picked it up from the ground outside and returned it to the holster earlier. He was calling himself all kinds of double-damned fool as he plucked the gun from its sheath.

"Here, now!" Stone caught at his good arm. "What the hell are you doin', Sam? You ain't in no shape to go rampagin' around—"

"I've got to stop her before she goes to see Croft," Cody snapped. "Don't you see, Caleb? He's no preacher. He's a goddamned gun smuggler!"

No, of course Stone didn't see, Cody realized. In fact, the wagon master was staring at him as if he'd taken leave of his senses. But Cody knew he was seeing things straight for the first time. He'd dismissed Josiah Croft as a suspect for a variety of reasons: the "minister's" friendship with Caleb Stone, which Cody had mistakenly taken for granted; the respect that the Ranger felt for a man of God, even though he himself wasn't particularly religious; maybe even the fact that Croft reminded him somewhat of his own commander, the hellfire-and-brimstone-spouting Captain Vickery. The only thing that mattered now, though, was that Cody had been wrong, and he knew without a doubt that underneath that screen of Bibles were more than two hundred stolen Winchesters.

Cody tucked the pistol behind his belt and pushed past Stone. Ignoring the pain in his arm and head, he threw a leg over the tailgate and hopped out of the wagon. Stone scrambled after him.

"Dammit, Cody, I don't know what sort of ideas you got in your head, but you're in no shape to be doin' this!"

"I've got to, Caleb," Cody grated as he strode across the camp. The people he passed gave him curious looks, but that didn't slow him down. Peering toward Croft's wagons, he looked for some sign of Angela—

There she was! She was standing behind one of the wagons, and Croft was beside her, his hand on her shoulder. He seemed to be urging her to get into the wagon. Cody couldn't let that happen.

"Angela!" he called.

She and Croft both jerked around, and when Cody saw her pale, taut face, he knew that she had already discovered Croft's guilt. He was reaching for his Colt as she cried out, "He's got the guns, Sam!"

Then she twisted in Croft's grasp and punched him in the throat as hard as she could.

The phony reverend staggered back a step, his grip loosening enough for Angela to wrench free. Croft rasped a curse and frantically dug under his coat for a gun. Cody was lifting his weapon, and the settlers between him and Croft suddenly got out of the way.

"Hold it, Croft!" Cody shouted. "In the name of the state of Texas, you're under arrest!"

Croft's rough-hewn features twisted into a snarling grimace as he brought out a pistol. The Ranger waited as long as he could, giving the gun smuggler a chance to surrender. But Croft wasn't going to surrender.

Cody fired a split second before his adversary. The bullet slammed Croft back against the wagon as his gun discharged harmlessly into the ground in front of him. With his free hand he clawed at the vehicle for a second, holding himself up and trying to raise the revolver for another shot. Croft's mouth opened, but all that came out was a bloody bubble; then he pitched forward onto his face.

Cody heard more guns going off and saw Croft's men emerging from the wagons, several of them firing to-

ward him. As he dropped to a knee he glanced around for
Angela and saw that she had rolled to relative safety under a wagon. Cody triggered a shot, and one of the smugglers spun crazily to the ground. Somewhere close beside
him, another pistol crashed. Caleb Stone was joining the
fight, even though he didn't know what was going on.
Even with Stone's help, though, Cody was badly outnum-
bered.

Help arrived from another source to even the odds.
Two rifles began barking from the other side of the
camp, and when Cody threw a look in that direction, he
saw Willard Morgan and Jasper Mertz joining the fight.
Their slugs cut down three more of Croft's men.

The fighting was fierce but short-lived. Within minutes, the gun smugglers—the ones left alive—had
thrown down their weapons and yelled out their surrender. Cody got wearily to his feet and walked toward
them, Caleb Stone at his side. Morgan and Mertz approached, too, covering the prisoners with their rifles,
while other men immediately cut lengths of rope to
bind the prisoners' hands.

With a shake of his head, Stone said quietly, "In the
name o' the state of Texas, eh? I reckon you got some
explainin' to do, Sam."

"I'm a Texas Ranger," Cody said, knowing that se-
crecy was no longer important. "Croft and his men
stole some rifles from the army and planned to sell
them to the Comanche."

Stone let out a curse of surprise. "You sure about
that?"

"I'm sure. If you look in those crates, under the Bibles, you'll find Winchesters."

"I'll have a look, all right," Stone said grimly, heading for the wagons.

Angela emerged from her hiding place and ran to
meet Cody. Still holding the revolver, he put his good
arm around her and asked softly, "Are you all right?"

She had her face pressed against his chest, and he
felt her nod. "I'm fine. You got here just in time. But
Sam, how did you know—"

"That Croft had the guns? More a hunch than anything else. Stone said he saw one of Croft's so-called converts using a brand-new Winchester during that comanchero raid, and that tipped me off."

Angela looked up at him and nodded again. "I stumbled on to him trying to hide the rifle in one of the crates, under a couple of layers of Bibles. They . . . they planned to kill me, Sam."

"Well, it's all over now," Cody said quietly. "Croft and his boys won't hurt anybody ever again. And those rifles will wind up where they're supposed to, not in the hands of the Indians."

Angela summoned up a smile. "Then our job is over."

"Soon as we deliver those Winchesters to Ranger headquarters in Del Rio so that they can be shipped back to the army."

From behind him Willard Morgan said, "That won't be necessary."

Cody looked around, frowning. With the prisoners taken care of, Morgan and his hired driver had strolled over to join Cody and Angela.

"I'll take possession of the weapons," the major went on. "After all, I represent the army in this matter, and the army owns those rifles."

Stone, who had climbed into one of the wagons to check on the crates, emerged in time to hear Morgan's statement. The wagon master scowled as he grumbled, "Sam's a Ranger and you're an army agent? Hell, is anybody on this train who they're supposed to be?"

Ignoring Stone's comment, Cody said to Morgan, "I think we'd better take the guns on to Del Rio, like I said. We can both be responsible for their safety till then, Major."

Morgan's smile lost some of its smooth assurance. "This isn't your decision to make. I'm taking charge of those guns. Mertz and I are turning around right now and heading back to San Antonio with them."

"By yourselves? What about those comancheros?"

Morgan waved a hand carelessly. "They won't

bother us, not after the beating they took this morning. We'll be fine."

Cody shook his head stubbornly and said, "I can't let you do it. You can argue with my captain when we get to Del Rio."

Suddenly, Morgan snapped up the barrel of the rifle he had been holding. Lining the weapon on Cody, he glowered and said, "I'm taking the rifles, dammit, and you won't stop me!"

Stone exclaimed, "What the hell!" and started to reach for his Remington.

But Jasper Mertz prodded the wagon master in the back with his rifle. "Don't try it, Stone," the driver growled.

Cody could hear his pulse hammering inside his head as he tightened his arm around Angela and stared angrily at Morgan. "Son of a bitch," the Ranger said. "You're not a major at all, are you?"

The Easterner smiled. "The closest I ever came to a major was when one threw me into the stockade once. I'm afraid the real Major Morgan is buried over near Hallettsville. That's where I ambushed him while he was on his way to San Antonio."

"And you stole his identification papers and took his place," Cody finished.

"That's right. We knew that those stolen rifles would probably be routed through San Antonio, and it was my job to find them before Croft and his men could get them to the Comanche."

"Who're you working with?" Cody demanded. "The comancheros?"

Morgan's smile widened into a leer. "Quite an astute deduction. Yes, Jasper and I work for the comancheros. We had already disposed of the man the army sent; once I figured out you were a Ranger, you had to be taken care of, too."

"So you did try to beat me to death," Cody muttered. He was watching for a chance to jump Morgan, but as long as the imposter kept his guard up, it would be too dangerous for Angela if Cody made a move against him.

"No, that was Jasper. We almost got rid of you that night, but Croft saved your bacon. Ironic, isn't it? You didn't know who he really was, and he had no idea you were a Ranger. Then the next day you somehow spotted me up on that ridge and got out of the way when I tried to shoot you. You're a lucky man, my friend. Obviously I wasn't interested in scaring you off. I wanted you dead."

"I told you before," Cody grated, "I'm not your friend."

Practically the whole camp had gathered around by now, but no one could do anything while Morgan and Mertz were menacing Cody, Angela, and Stone with their rifles. It was a standoff, and Stone said to Morgan, "You don't really reckon you can get out of here, do you, mister? Ever'body's heard now about them rifles and how you plan to sell 'em to the Comanch'. These folks ain't goin' to let you leave, and the two of you sure can't kill all of us."

"We won't have to." Morgan's expression became maddeningly smug, and Cody ached to smash it off his face. "We have friends." He pointed.

Somehow Cody knew what he was going to see even before he turned and looked, but he felt compelled to confirm his guess, so he wheeled around, taking Angela with him, and stared toward the ridge about a half mile distant that Morgan was indicating. Figures on horseback waited there, a hundred or more on fast, sleek ponies. The distance was too great for him to make out details, but he knew they would be wearing warbonnets and paint. Among them were white men, the survivors of the early morning raid on the wagon train, Cody guessed.

"I knew when our men failed this morning, they would fall back on our second plan," Morgan gloated. "They've joined forces with the Comanches who were planning to meet the train and buy the rifles from Croft. It won't matter to the Indians who supplies the guns. They're willing to pay whoever has the Winchesters. So my friends and I will wind up rich men after all."

Cody stared at the distant force of Indians and renegade whites. They were sitting calmly, waiting . . . Waiting for what?

The signal to attack.

Cody twisted around, pulling his injured arm out of the sling and forcing it to work long enough to shove Angela out of the way. He saw the mirror that Morgan was slipping out of his pocket and lunged toward the secret comanchero as Morgan started to lift the glass. "No!" Cody shouted.

He was too late. The late morning sun reflected off the mirror, sending a brilliant flash of light out toward the Indians and comancheros. A second later, Cody smashed into Morgan, knocking the renegade's Winchester aside and shattering the glass with a swipe of his pistol barrel. In a continuation of the same movement, Cody chopped at Morgan's head with the gun.

Jasper Mertz swung the barrel of his rifle toward the grappling pair, and that was all the break Caleb Stone needed. The wagon master's hand dipped to his gun, fingers curling around the butt of the Remington and lifting it smoothly from the holster. Mertz tried to switch his aim back to Stone, but before he could, the Remington boomed. Mertz was jarred back a step by the slug that tore through his body just below the right shoulder. Losing his balance, he sat down hard.

Morgan drove the butt of his rifle into Cody's belly. The Ranger grunted in pain and lost his grip on the renegade, who then leapt back and brought the gun to bear on Cody again. Cody tried to raise his pistol, but he knew he wasn't going to make it in time to keep Morgan from getting off a shot.

The crack of another gun sounded sharply in the clearing in the circle of wagons.

With a cry of pain Morgan stared down at the blood that had suddenly appeared on his shirtfront. He

blinked, tried to say something, then crumpled lifelessly to the ground.

Cody looked around and saw Angela Halliday, in her
hand Josiah Croft's fallen pistol that she had scooped
up from the ground.

Stone stepped forward quickly and kicked the rifle
out of Mertz's hands. "Reckon that'll do it for these
two," he said. "That was nice shootin', Mrs. Cole—or
whatever your name is, ma'am."

Cody nodded in agreement. His eyes met Angela's,
and he said simply, "Thank you." She smiled at him,
then lowered the pistol with a trembling hand, and
Cody knew that now that the immediate threat was
over, reaction was setting in.

But he wouldn't be able to comfort her now, the
Ranger thought as he glanced out over the plains to the
north. The combined force of Indians and comancheros was still sweeping toward them. "Caleb!" he
said sharply. "Break out those rifles from Croft's wagons! There should be plenty of ammunition with them.
Pass them out to all the men on the train—the women,
too! We're not out of the woods yet."

"Not by a damn sight," Stone concurred as he signaled to some of his scouts to get in the wagons and
start handing out the army rifles. The attackers would
be in range in a matter of minutes. Already the onrushing marauders were firing their own guns and uttering
chilling, bloodthirsty yells.

Angela caught at Cody's right arm as he started past
her. "You're bleeding!" she exclaimed. "Your wound
must have opened up again."

Cody did feel a little dizzy, but there wasn't time to
worry about that. "It'll just have to wait," he told her,
reaching up to take one of the repeating rifles that
Stone's men were handing down from the wagons. He
tucked the Colt behind his belt and took a handful of
cartridges for the Winchester. Glancing at Angela
again, he saw the strength and resolution on her face
and knew that he wouldn't have to worry about her

going into hysterics. Not this time and maybe never again.

She looked up at the scout in the wagon and said calmly, "Give me one of those rifles."

Cody ran to the spot between two of the prairie schooners where Stone had stationed himself, noticing that all along the wagon train, the settlers were filling the gaps and loading the new weapons. Glancing right and left, the Ranger saw the way the settlers were preparing to face this battle, and he grinned. Those Indians and renegades were in for a hell of a surprise.

Angela appeared beside him, rifle in hand, and returned his grin. "You ready, Ranger?" she asked lightly.

"Ready, ma'am," Cody replied. Bullets thudded into the dirt on the other side of the wagons and occasionally whined overhead as the raiders came within rifle range.

"Let's start the ball!" shouted Caleb Stone.

Cody brought the Winchester to his shoulder, settled the sights on one of the warbonneted warriors, then pressed the trigger. The rifle cracked, bucking back against his shoulder. He saw the Comanche brave go spinning off his horse, but before the Indian hit the ground, Cody had worked the lever, shifted his sights, and fired again. All along the line of wagons, men and women were doing the same, defending with their lives all of the hopes and dreams that had brought them here.

If there were time to concentrate on anything else, Cody thought fleetingly as he fired, jacked the Winchester's lever, and fired again, he would've felt downright proud to be among them.

But right now there was a job to be done. . . .

CHAPTER
IIIIIIIIIIIIIIIIIIIIIIIII **13** IIIIIIIIIIIIIIIIIIIIIIIII

The wagon train rolled into Del Rio two days later, somewhat the worse for wear. Most of the vehicles sported quite a few bullet holes in their canvas. Some of them were driven by grim-faced women who'd lost their men in the battle with the Indians and the comancheros. One wagon was full of prisoners who were turned over to Sheriff Christian Burke to hold until somebody could figure out whether Texas or the army had first call on them. The dead men—including Josiah Croft and Willard Morgan—had been buried on the trail after the attackers had been routed . . . which was more than Croft and Morgan deserved, as far as Cody was concerned.

Though the Ranger's left arm was still pretty sore, he was convinced it was going to heal all right, and his headaches were much better. He felt almost human again after this rough assignment, and he had only one major worry now: What the hell was he going to do about Angela Halliday?

She had all but said that she loved him. He had told her that there was no place in his life for a wife, not as long as he was a Ranger. Besides, she had suffered the pain of losing one lawman husband. Surely she wouldn't want to risk going through that again.

Those thoughts were running through his mind as he walked from the sheriff's office toward Ranger headquarters, accompanied by Captain Wallace Vickery. The blustery old commandant glanced over at him and said, "Son, you look like you got the weight of the world on your shoulders. Hell's bells, boy, I thought you'd be happy with the way you wrapped up this little chore!"

"I'm fine, Cap'n," Cody said with a sad smile. "I've just got a few things on my mind."

"That gal from San Antone, I reckon," Vickery said sagely. "Well, Cody, when it comes to womenfolk, you got to do what's in your heart. It's not always easy to figure out what that is, but you got to try." He put his hand on Cody's shoulder. "I'd sure hate to lose you as a Ranger, but I reckon you'll do whatever's best."

Cody wished he were that certain.

As he emerged from headquarters an hour later, after giving Vickery all the details of the mission, an eastbound stagecoach was just pulling up in front of the stage line office. A woman emerged from the building, her brightly colored clothes and hat catching Cody's attention. He stopped in his tracks, eyes widening as he stared at her. It was Angela Halliday.

She was wearing an outfit that would do justice to the Crystal Slipper, a low-cut silk gown and a neat little hat with a spray of plumage on top of it. Several men came out of the stage station and clustered around her, and from across the street, Cody heard her merry laugh as she joked with them. He felt a peculiar tightness in his chest at the sound, but then it passed and he put a smile on his face as he started over toward her.

"Well," he said in a dry voice as he came up behind her, "looks like I got a divorce without even knowing it."

She turned to face him, and even though there was a bright smile on her lips, he thought he caught a momentary glimpse of sadness in her eyes. "Hello, Sam," she said.

"Did you figure on leaving without saying goodbye?"

"I . . . thought it might be best."

Cody glanced at the other men standing around, and suddenly they all seemed to decide it might be better to go ahead and board the coach. When he and Angela were alone on the boardwalk, he began, "I'm not sure what to say. . . ."

"Then don't say anything." She leaned closer to him, and her lips brushed his. As she stepped back, her eyes sparkling moistly, she added, "You come see me the next time you get to San Antonio, you hear? Drinks're on the house"—her smile broadened into the bawdy grin he remembered so well—"and I'll show you one hell of a time, cowboy. I might even break my rule for you."

"Sure." Cody grinned back at her. Abruptly, he pulled her back into his arms, gave her a resounding kiss, and then turned her toward the coach. "So long, darlin'."

His hand slapped sharply against her rump as she climbed aboard. If that was the way she wanted to play it—if it was easier on her this way—then it was fine with him, too. He knew he'd probably never visit her again . . . but he'd never forget her, either.

He turned on his heel and strode away.

As he headed for his room at the Rio Grande Hotel, he remembered that Captain Vickery had said something about a chore that needed doing over Big Bend way. As soon as his arm was a little better, he'd be ready to ride.

CODY'S LAW: BOOK 3

BORDER SHOWDOWN

by Matthew S. Hart

Returning to headquarters from a routine patrol, Texas Ranger Sam Cody quells an attack by bandits on a covered wagon and rescues the travelers, three Easterners on a photographic expedition throughout the West—an elderly professor, his young niece, and his assistant. To fund their journey, the threesome have been setting up their equipment in towns along the way, where citizens turn out in droves to have their pictures taken. When the novelty of having their images captured for posterity draws three elusive desperadoes out of hiding, which enables the Rangers to help them meet an untimely end, Cody gets an idea: He'll travel with the Easterners undercover as their guide, with a Ranger troop trailing at a reasonable distance; whenever outlaws are flushed out of hiding, the Rangers will swoop in and make arrests. After Cody's commanding officer approves the plan, the journey begins.

The Ranger begins to suspect that a mastermind is overseeing various gangs in the region, organizing them into a cohesive force. Soon the finger points to Normal Parnell, a successful entrepreneur in Brackettville. Cody gains an entrée to a local gang, and he soon knows the plans for several holdups. Evidence against Parnell quickly mounts—but before Cody can prove his hunch, the tables are turned in a deadly double-cross.

Read BORDER SHOWDOWN, on sale December 1991 wherever Bantam Books are sold.

★ WAGONS WEST ★

This continuing, magnificent saga recounts the adventures of a brave band of settlers, all of different backgrounds, all sharing one dream—to find a new and better life.

- ☐ 26822-8   INDEPENDENCE! #1 .... $4.95
- ☐ 26162-2   NEBRASKA! #2 .... $4.95
- ☐ 26242-4   WYOMING! #3 .... $4.95
- ☐ 26072-3   OREGON! #4 .... $4.50
- ☐ 26070-7   TEXAS! #5 .... $4.99
- ☐ 26377-3   CALIFORNIA! #6 .... $4.99
- ☐ 26546-6   COLORADO! #7 .... $4.95
- ☐ 26069-3   NEVADA! #8 .... $4.99
- ☐ 26163-0   WASHINGTON! #9 .... $4.50
- ☐ 26073-1   MONTANA! #10 .... $4.95
- ☐ 26184-3   DAKOTA! #11 .... $4.50
- ☐ 26521-0   UTAH! #12 .... $4.50
- ☐ 26071-5   IDAHO! #13 .... $4.50
- ☐ 26367-6   MISSOURI! #14 .... $4.50
- ☐ 27141-5   MISSISSIPPI! #15 .... $4.95
- ☐ 25247-X   LOUISIANA! #16 .... $4.50
- ☐ 25622-X   TENNESSEE! #17 .... $4.50
- ☐ 26022-7   ILLINOIS! #18 .... $4.95
- ☐ 26533-4   WISCONSIN! #19 .... $4.95
- ☐ 26849-X   KENTUCKY! #20 .... $4.95
- ☐ 27065-6   ARIZONA! #21 .... $4.99
- ☐ 27458-9   NEW MEXICO! #22 .... $4.95
- ☐ 27703-0   OKLAHOMA! #23 .... $4.95
- ☐ 28180-1   CELEBRATION! #24 .... $4.50

Bantam Books, Dept. LE, 414 East Golf Road, Des Plaines, IL 60016

Please send me the items I have checked above. I am enclosing $_____
(please add $2.50 to cover postage and handling). Send check or money order, no cash or C.O.D.s please.

Mr/Ms _____

Address _____

City/State _____ Zip _____

Please allow four to six weeks for delivery.
Prices and availability subject to change without notice.   LE-9/91